Charles Mathew Clode

London during the Great Rebellion

Being a Memoir of Sir Abraham Reynardson

Charles Mathew Clode

London during the Great Rebellion
Being a Memoir of Sir Abraham Reynardson

ISBN/EAN: 9783337209599

Printed in Europe, USA, Canada, Australia, Japan

Cover: Foto ©Raphael Reischuk / pixelio.de

More available books at **www.hansebooks.com**

London during the Great Rebellion.

BEING A MEMOIR OF

Sir ABRAHAM REYNARDSON, Knt.,

SHERIFF, AND MASTER OF THE MERCHANT TAYLORS'
COMPANY, 1640-41.

LORD MAYOR OF LONDON.

Elected 1648; Dismissed 1649; Re-elected 1660.

By CHARLES M. CLODE, F.S.A.

(Master 1873-74).

LONDON:

HARRISON AND SONS, ST. MARTIN'S LANE,
Printers in Ordinary to Her Majesty.

1892.

PREFACE.

Perhaps it may be well that I should explain in a few lines how it is that this memoir appears.

Some time since the Merchant Taylors' Company purchased the portrait of Sir Abraham Reynardson, and were then *informed* that as the Lord Mayor of London in 1648 he had refused—having regard to the oaths he had taken—to proclaim the abolition of the Kingly office. It then appeared to me that the other incidents in the life of such a man, if they could be recovered, would be worth preserving; and knowing as I do how the Company cherish the memories of those worthies who in historic times have filled their chair, I devoted such leisure as I have to make search for these, and the result is to be found in the following pages.

It is seldom that a citizen, even in eventful times, leaves, or that his family or descendants otherwise possess any materials for history. These are to be sought for elsewhere; if he has served his fellow-citizens in high office, first in the records of his Guild and then of the Corporation. But to bear their full meaning these materials must be illustrated by placing on the text a statement of the circumstances (civic or political) which give to his actions their due weight and importance. In this manner the memoir becomes a Chapter in the history of the Guild or Corporation, and where, as in this instance, the times are those of crises—of London—each phase commanding a wider interest than that of mere personal act or character.

If this view be correct it will supply the excuse, should such be needed, for this publication.

While Reynardson was connected with the Corporation great events were dealt with. In 1640 the invasion of the Scots obliged the King to raise the first loan from the Livery Companies. In 1642 Parliament was obliged to raise the second loan from them to suppress the rebellion in Ireland. In 1643 the approach of the King's forces towards London induced the Corporation to raise the third loan from them—loans, let it be said, never repaid, and the negotiations for which illustrate the methods and difficulties of borrowing money for public purposes before the constitutional period of 1688.

Years of trouble accumulated until they reached a climax during Reynardson's mayoralty in 1648. Then it was—in his six months' tenure of office—that he acted so heroic a part on behalf of his fellow-citizens in valiantly resisting "turbulent disorders" and the intended policy of the Rump to involve the Corporation of London in their criminal course of bringing their King to the scaffold.

As the resolute attitude of Reynardson upon the 13th January has never attracted the notice of any writer, although at the time of the Restoration the Corporation of London intended to do full justice to him in their "Vindication of the Conduct of the City" which they put forth to the world, I have endeavoured to collect the facts leading up to the crisis, so that the citizens of this generation may decide for themselves whether or not he deserves the praise that was bestowed upon him by his contemporaries, and was one of "those famous men" who have been "the glory of their times."

London, June, 1892.

ANALYSIS OF CONTENTS.

PAGE

B

NOTE TO THE REFERENCES AS UNDER.

(*a*) The MS. Records of the London Corporation.

(*b*) The MS. Records (vol. 9) of the Merchant Taylors' Company.

(*bb*) The MS. Records of the Grocers' Company.

(*c*) The MS. Records of St. Bartholomew's Hospital.

(*d*) The Calendar (Domestic Series) of State Papers (1640–65).

(*e*) The Commons' Journals (1640–65).

(*f*) The Parliamentary History (31 vols. London, 1672—1803).

(*g*) Rushworth's Historical Collection (2nd ed., 1721).

(*h*) Whitelock's Memorials (London, 1732).

> The above authorities, being compiled in chronological order, can be referred to by the date given in the text.

(*i*) Memorials of the Merchant Taylors' Company. London, 1875.

(*j*) Early History of the Merchant Taylors' Company, with Notes of the Lives of some of its Eminent Members. By C. M. Clode. London, Harrison and Sons, 1888.

(*k*) The State Trials (vols. 4 and 5) of 21 vols. 8vo. By John Howell, F.S.A.

(*l*) History of the Great Civil War, 1640–50. By S. A. Gardiner.

LONDON DURING THE GREAT REBELLION.

ABRAHAM REYNARDSON was born at Plymouth in the year 1590,[1] and was the son of Thomas Reynardson by Julia, his wife, whose surname was Brace, living in the Isle of Wight. The father was one of the principal merchants[2] in the West of England, and he, with others of that town, entered into an agreement of the 14th January, 1613, to defray the expenses of a prosecution for extortion to be undertaken against the Customs Officers there. The son came to London for his apprenticeship to Edmund James, of the Merchant Taylors' Company (b), and became a freeman of London on the 5th of October, 1618.

His first wife was Abigail, the third daughter of Sir Nicholas Crispe,[3] of Bread Street, who was one of the leading Royalists, and is described by Clarendon "as a citizen of good wealth, great trade, and an active-spirited man," and was welcomed by Charles I to Oxford, in 1643, as "his little old faithful farmer."

His earlier life was passed in the parish of St. Andrew Undershaft, where the children of his first marriage were born, and this wife died in July, 1632.[4] His two elder sons were scholars in the Company's School, but Nicholas (his second son), born in April, 1630, was the only child of this marriage who survived his parents.[5]

His second wife was Eleanor, the daughter of Richard Wynne, of Shrewsbury, of which marriage there were six children living at the time of his decease. One of these, Samuel, the eldest son, was born in the parish of St. Martin Outwich, in March, 1638, and entered as a scholar of the Company's School in 1647-48.

---

[1] Robinson's Tottenham, vol. 1, page 103.

[2] 10th Report H.M.S., page 548.

[3] London, Visitation, vol. 1, page 202; his Life, D. N. B., vol. 13, page 95; Clar. Reb., vol. 4, page 63 (Oxford, 826).

[4] It is not easy to reconcile the statements in the Visitation of London, 1633-34 (vol. 2, page 198), with the register of St. Andrew Undershaft. The latter gives the date as quoted (Robinson, vol. 1, page 167). Reynardson had two Samuels; one died and was buried at St. Andrew's, 20th December, 1631, and the other buried his father (*ibid.*, page 184).

[5] Appendix III.

His first advancement in his Guild was his election in December, 1625, to the office of "Warden-Substitute of the Bachelors' Company of the Merchant Taylors' quarter," which he gained on scrutiny against John Wilford,[1] whose family had an established position in the City. From this office he was taken into the Livery, in 1626, paying, because of his tenure as Warden-Substitute, the lesser fee of 35s., which was given in part (5s. 3d.) to the Master and the rest to the officials.

In 1639 he purchased the freehold mansion house on the north side of Tottenham Green, which was standing at the commencement of the present century,[2] and in 1640 he took an assignment of Sir W. Acton's house in Bishopsgate Street, belonging to the Company, formerly occupied by Lord Wriottesley, Henry VIII's Chancellor.[3]

Of the other incidents of his domestic life we know little; but his character and virtues are described with some fulness of detail by one who had many years' acquaintance with him—probably living adjacent to him in St. Martin's parish, and who preached his funeral sermon.[4] It is sufficient here to say that he was a stanch English churchman, and "that the stream of his bounty did run chiefly in one channel, viz.: in taking poor children and placing them in such callings wherein they might get their own bread."

We must turn, therefore, to his public life as a citizen in the eventful period in which he bore a part, so far as it can be traced upon the records of the Corporation and of the Merchant Taylors' Company.

When he entered upon the political arena, Charles I had

---

[1] See Wilford, in Index to the Early History of the Merchant Taylors' Company, 1888.

[2] Lysons' Environs, vol. 3, page 547. Robinson has an engraving of the house, vol. 2, page 102.

[3] In 1640 Reynardson took an assignment of Sir William Acton's lease of "a messuage and three tenements" in Bishopsgate Street, which had previously been in the tenure of the Earl of Warwick, at a rent of 14l. a year, and in 1644 a lease of another property, described as "a great messuage and two tenements" in Bishopsgate Street, "some time in the occupation of Lord Wriothesley, Lord Chancellor of England," at a rent of 10l. a year. Both these leases were surrendered in 1644, and a new lease of the whole plot, at a rent of 24l. a year, was granted to Reynardson for 45 years from Michaelmas, 1644. This lease was surrendered in 1647, and a new lease was granted to Reynardson for 55 years from Michaelmas, 1647.

[4] Appendix II, sermon by George Smallwood, 17th October, 1661 (Brit. Mus. Col., 226-$\frac{9}{2}$-23). He attested his will, and Matthew was the rector of St. Martin's from 1634 to 1674.

rendered himself unpopular with the citizens, and especially by his confiscation of their Ulster estates. He had governed for 11 years in an arbitrary manner without a Parliament. Things were out of joint, and it was difficult to get the citizens to accept the higher offices in the Corporation. Consequently, in 1639, at the election of Sheriffs, between the 8th and 24th of July, Reynardson and 12 others were elected and discharged without fine. On the 31st 16 others were chosen, ending the list with John Warner, the Grocer (of whom we shall hear much hereafter), who accepted office as Sheriff for the year.[1]

Reynardson's election, although he was discharged from serving, as Sheriff, brought him on to the Court of the Merchant Taylors in August, and on the 14th July of the following year (1640) he was chosen Master.

This election was, for what reason I know not, made "in as private a manner as conveniently might be," no public guests (save the Master and Wardens of the Skynners) being invited, no publication of the election being made, nor garlands offered. In the same month he was again elected Sheriff (one Rogers having been previously discharged from the offices of Sheriff and Alderman by the payment of 800*l*.), but he appeared on the 16th to ask for exemption by fine, thus :—" Item: this day Abraham Reynoldson, Esq., citizen and Merchant Taylor of London, of late elected by the Commons of this City to be one of the Sheriffs of this City and County of Middlesex for the year ensuing, made his personal appearance before this Court, and refused to seal a bond of 1,000*l*., with condition to take upon him the office and charge of the said place of shrievalty on the Vigil of St. Michael the Archangel now next ensuing; but for his discharge desired to be admitted to his fine imposed by Act of Common Council; whereupon this Court, taking into consideration the said Mr. Reynoldson and his request, as also the necessity of having a Sheriffe, did not at present think fit to give way thereunto" (*a*). However, on the 21st, he determined to accept office, and entered into his bond for its due discharge.

As Sheriff he could have claimed exemption from the " Mastership ;" but on the 23rd September, at the earnest request of the Court, " he lovingly declared that, notwithstanding his earnest engagement and employment, he was willing to do the Company all the service he could, and would hold the place of Master, which favour the Court thankfully acknowledged."

---

[1] *a.* With the sanction of Dr. Sharpe, of the Guildhall, Mr. Chambers, of the Merchant Taylors' Company, has kindly made these extracts for me.

While the incidents which we have described were happening in the City, Charles had to summon his fourth Parliament, and, being therein arraigned for his illegal acts, had dissolved it on the 6th May, 1640. But the King soon became in need of money, and Reynardson's Mastership is memorable for one incident at least,[1] viz., the initiation of those loans (three in number) which were obtained from, and *are still due* to, the Livery Companies.

The first loan was made to the King, the second to Parliament, and the third to the city of London. Each varied in its political interest, and by contrasting the action of the Merchant Taylors' with the Grocers' Company (who have favoured me with a copy of their Court minutes), we shall detect in these two instances the political sympathy which each Company evinced towards the King or Parliament.

It must be borne in mind, as indeed it will be seen, that though London was the place and the citizens the persons where and by whom loans were made, yet that in Charles I's reign an essential difference existed at that and the present period as to the method and facility of raising a loan.[2] Then there was no open market for money; no bank with a gold reserve; no paper currency; no public funds; no shares in any private enterprise[3] to be easily realised in cash. What the King had to find were those of his subjects who had gold, plate, or precious stones, which they were able and willing to lend to him as an ordinary debtor giving good security.

The King's first attempt to reach these was by private negotiation with the Lord Mayor, and then through the Council Board. From the news letters written to Lord Conway (*d*, page 31), we have an insight into the King's pecuniary needs, and his attempts to supply them.

On the 14th April Rosingham writes that the Lord Mayor had been three times to the King about a loan of 100,000*l.* from the Bench of Aldermen, but that the King, finding it impossible to get the money from them, had consented that the Lord Mayor

---

[1] The Merchant Taylors' Company have Reynardson's signature to the audited accounts and to the appointment to a Scholarship at St. John's of William Hardinge, who took arms against the Parliament, and was expelled by the Visitors in 1648 (School Register, vol. 1, page 144, note 9).

[2] See Cunningham's Industry and Commerce (1890), pages 315—333.

[3] The New River Company was divided into 72 shares, 36 of which were in the hands of 29 adventurers, who were incorporated on the 21st of June, 1612, and might sell if a purchaser could have been found. Charles I had transferred his 36 shares to the second Sir Hugh Myddelton.

should take in what rich Commoners he could, provided the Common Council were not consulted. Nothing came of this permission, and the next meeting (with the Lord Mayor and half the Bench of Aldermen) was at the Bishop of London's Palace, where (he notices), as an incident of civic etiquette, that "the Lord Mayor sat with his hat on, and the sword before him." Alderman Bromfield was challenged with having offered a loan of 3,700*l.* last summer, but this he denied; whereupon the Lords of the Council sought to impose on him a loan of 2,000*l.*, but he refused "to lend above 1,000*l.*, and that upon good security." Again the meeting failed, so that the Lord Mayor and *all* the Aldermen were to appear at the Council Office before the King. Upon their appearing he declared his necessity was so great at present, that he must borrow of the City 100,000*l.*, at 8*l.* per cent., which, if lent, would do him more good than 20 subsidies. After the King's speech was delivered, the Lord Privy Seal told the Lord Mayor and Aldermen that the City was rather beholden to his Majesty for taking their money than that the King should be beholden to the City for lending it. But the citizens failed to see the matter in this light, and no business was done (*d*, page 155, (24)).

In May the subject was renewed by the King, when the Lord Mayor and all the Aldermen were summoned to the Council, and told that because they had not provided 100,000*l.*, therefore the King now required 200,000*l.*, and demanded a list of the names of rich men in every ward by Sunday, or that he would have 300,000*l.* of the City; but though they appeared on Sunday, it was only to pray of the Board to be excused from supplying such lists; yet, when all the Aldermen apart were asked for such they consented to give it, save four Aldermen, who refused thus to betray their fellow citizens, and suffered imprisonment, viz., Sir Nicholas Raynton,[1] in the Marshalsea; Alderman Soames, in the Fleet; Alderman Atkins, in the King's Bench; and Alderman Gayre, in the Gate House.

Such were the King's negotiations for a loan, and therefore, as they failed absolutely, he sought in June to obtain an assessment (*d*, page 308) upon the citizens for the pay of the Army, but met with a refusal as the expenditure was beyond the City area. Being in desperate need, in July he created a panic on the Exchange by seizing all the bullion sent to the Tower, principally by the Spanish merchants for coinage, and of which he restored only a part,

---

[1] A portrait of this citizen hangs on the wall of the Treasurer's Office in St. Bartholomew's Hospital.

keeping one-third as a loan, upon such security as he offered to them and they thought it expedient to accept.

The King's next application[1] to the Corporation for a loan met with no success, as the Common Council alleged that they had no authority from their fellow citizens to use the credit of their Common Seal for such a purpose. A suggestion was then thrown out and acted upon unsuccessfully by the Lord Mayor; viz., that the several Livery Companies who had on other occasions lent money and been repaid by the Crown should be asked for money. It appears from the Grocers' records that the Lord Mayor wrote on July 28th to the Master and Wardens stating that 5,000*l*. had been allotted to them as a loan to the King, and requesting that, if not satisfied with the security or any other matter, they would repair to him. On the 31st the Court decided to send and make answer to the Lord Mayor by "word of mouth" that they declined to make the advance. A similar application and with the same result was, I believe, made to the Mercers; but the Merchant Taylors' Company's records contain no entry upon the subject.

The King's necessities became even more urgent as public disasters were arising; the Scots crossed the Border into England on the 20th August (*f*, vol. 3, pages 216—222, 259—263), and were living at free quarter in the northern counties of Northumberland and Durham. Knowing how the King would ask the aid of the citizens against them, the Scots wrote on the 9th September to the Corporation, who as a consequence sent a deputation of citizens to York with a petition from their whole body, praying the King for a Parliament and for peace; he had therefore no alternative than to call a Parliament (the fifth and Long Parliament of his reign), and, as matters were urgent, he summoned the Peers as a *quasi*-representative body to meet him at York.

Upon their assembling in the hall of the Deanery[2] there, he laid before them petitions from Durham and Northumberland for relief from the free quarters of the Scottish Army, and addressed them on the aspect of public affairs. As the result of the meeting the Peers determined upon the policy to be carried out, viz., that the King should make another application to the City for money by his sign manual letter, and that they should support his application by a letter from themselves, offering to be responsible for the repayment of 200,000*l*., which was the loan required.

---

[1] The impeachment of the Recorder (Gardiner) for his advice on this application, *k*, page 109.

[2] Drake's Eboracum, page 140; *g*, vol. 3, page 1275; *f*, vol. 2, page 389.

A sub-committee of Peers was appointed to draft their letter to "Our very loving Friends, the Lord Mayor, Aldermen, Citizens, and Commonalty of the City of London," which was ultimately signed by 61 Peers, whose names are given at the foot.[1]

This letter, after stating the position of public affairs and referring to the loan, continued thus (*b*, page 117):—"That we are also so confident of H.M.'s royal performance that we offer ourselves to join in any further security as shall be agreed upon by the Lords (acting as a deputation) and yourselves."

Another committee of five Peers[2] had been appointed to take this letter to London, and negotiate "all particulars, both for security and days of payment, which may suit both to His Majesty's occasions and your own convenience." Accordingly, upon their arrival, they attended the Privy Council on the 1st of

---

[1] *i*, vol. 3, page 1279. The Peers' letter is not dated. It is signed by the following as entered on (*b*):—

John Finch Co.	Montague.
H. Manchester.	Conway and Kilvert.
Pembroke and Montgomery.	Campden.
Shrewsbury.	Audley.
Fras. Bedford.	Mowbray and Matravers.
Willm. Hartford.	J. Clifford.
Winchester.	Tho. Arundell.
Ro. Essex.	Strange.
T. Lincolne.	Willm. Sturtall.
Salisbury.	Tho. Windsor.
J. Bridgwater.	Wharton.
Northampton.	Willoughby.
Warwick.	Willm. Paggett.
W. Devonshire.	Du. Northey.
Hamilton, Earle of Cambridge.	Mandevile.
J. Looney, Earl of March.	Feildinge.
Denbigh.	Gray.
Bristol.	Faulkenbridge.
Holland.	Ja. Lovelace.
Clare.	Pawlett.
Hen. Dover.	Brudenell.
Peterborough.	W. Maynard.
Bullingbrooke.	Tho. Coventry.
Westmoreland.	Edw. Howard.
Berkshire.	Goringe.
Cleveland.	Savile.
Monmouth.	Dunsmere.
St. Ford St. Albans and Clenrickard.	Newport.
	Ro. Brooke.
Portland.	Carnarven.
Strafford.	

[2] These Peers were—Earls of Manchester and Pembroke, Viscount Campden, Lords Goring and Coventry.—*d*, pages 89—101.

October, to explain the object of their mission and their desire to ascertain whether the City would make the advance without the tender of the security, which they had authority to give (*d*, pages 128—133). A letter was therefore written to the Lord Mayor for a Common Council to be summoned, "none coming to it but such as ought."

On the 2nd the Peers went to the Guildhall to meet the Lord Mayor and Aldermen, to read the King's and the Peers' letters to them, and, above all, to obtain their sanction to the loan before meeting the Common Council, but the Lord Mayor and Aldermen cautiously refused to commit themselves, "until they saw how it would take with the Commons." The meeting was closed that the Peers might dine with the Lord Mayor, and, at three o'clock, attend the Common Council summoned to meet them.

The citizens, as we shall observe, were not unfrequently summoned by the Lord Mayor to determine political matters on very short notice. The oath of the members of the Common Council[1] pledged them "to come quickly when summoned; not to depart without license, nor to disclose what was there spoken." The citizens came to the Common Hall by summons from the several Masters of the several Guilds, but others, such as apprentices, not unfrequently came, though not entitled to vote. In the meeting about to be described, the Peers had desired that others than those who were members of the Common Council should be present, so that they had something more than a Common Council and less than a Common Hall; but, at either assembly, Reynardson, as Sheriff, would be present.

What occurred at this meeting of citizens is graphically told by the Peers, who reported their proceedings to the King (*d*). "We first read the letter from the Lords, which we discerned was well relished by them all. To back that, and to take off the excuse which with good manners they might make, how they could grant at the desire of the Lords what they had denied to your Majesty, we read your Majesty's letter, which gave them all ample satisfaction and removed all scruples." Other points were urged, and the Bishop of Durham's letter read, showing how the Scottish Army had used him. "These things being so lively represented to them as we could, made those impressions on them that we discerned as they sat, how well they were disposed to what we came about." The Peers "then withdrew, that they might more freely debate upon the ways of raising the sum desired; for we persuaded our-

---

[1] The Government of London.—*j*, page 16.

selves it would not be denied." Accordingly that night before the meeting broke up, " they resolved unanimously to grant what we desired, holding it so honourable, just, and necessary for the City to do, that no man so much as murmured about it."

The citizens so resolving were not accepting the loan themselves, but, save as they might be Liverymen transferring a bad security for a loan to others, for they held " the best and speediest way of raising the money to be to go to the Companies," and accordingly the Lord Mayor and Aldermen drafted a letter to be sent to them which we shall now notice :—

I. The loan of 50,000*l.* to Charles I.

Having seen how this loan was initiated at the Guildhall, we must now follow the subject into the Court Room of the Merchant Taylors' Company.

On the 3rd October the Lord Mayor wrote to the Merchant Taylors thus. First, he described the constitution of the Assembly : " I and my brethren the Aldermen having yesterday assembled ourselves together, the major part of the Common Councilmen, and many other of the best rank and quality, in the Chamber of the Guildhall, London." Then he explained the crisis in the north, and suggested a loan of 200,000*l.* to the King to be made; viz., 50,000*l.* on the 12th inst., 100,000*l.* on the 15th November next, 50,000*l.* on the 1st of December following (*b*, page 117).

The letter then continued :—" That after mature consideration held by us, the Lords being absent, of the whole contents of those letters and of what the Lords had pleased to acquaint us with . . . I . . . with an unanimous consent of the Lord Mayor and Aldermen, and the Assembly . . . have thought fit, by this my letter, to recommend this great and weighty cause to your serious care and consideration ; desiring you with a convenient expedition to take such effectual courses by your best furtherance as to the sum of 5,000*l.*, that, according to the usual proportion allotted upon the Company for corn, there may be raised by your Company towards the sum of 50,000*l.* which is to be lent on such security as is offered by their Lordships' letter, to be paid by the 12th instant. And so I bid you heartily farewell, and rest.

" HENRY GARRAWAY."[1]

The King, as the letters show, was to give such security as he had to offer, and he avowed " that he would sell himself to his

---

[1] See his Life, Dict. of N. B. (vol. 21, page 18), by Wm. Welch, F.S.A.

shirt for the Peers' indemnity." The Queen was also "content to yield anything," which some persons supposed to mean her jewels (*d*, pages 146—151); but the Lord Mayor was to ascertain what security the King could give. It appeared that the Crown revenues were not available; the customs, not for four years; imports of all kinds, some in three, others in two years; and that the profits of the Court of Wards, 70,000*l*. or 80,000*l*., after two years.

As the difficulty had never been with the citizens—having no money—but with the King having no security which they could accept, the negotiation was not much advanced by these disclosures, for the Lord Mayor doubted whether the citizens would accept the security which was thus disclosed. He therefore suggested that 100,000*l*. of the Queen's jewels should be pledged, and that five other, should be added to the five deputed, peers who should give a bond, to be prepared by the Recorder, for repayment of the loan, with 8*l*. per cent. interest, on the 30th October, 1641 (*d*, page 159).

At a later period the City assured the Queen that they had no desire to take her jewels in pledge, and the Peers, as the King's sureties, said "that they would have none of them " (*d*).

The subject must therefore be brought before each Guild separately to make the advance if its resources enabled it to do so.

As to the Merchant Taylors' resources, it may be stated that when Reynardson became Master he had handed over to him from the retiring Master 2,400*l*. in cash, liable to "trust" claims, as no distinction was then made between trust and corporate cash. He had bonds for money, lent to liverymen and others at 8*l*. per cent., for (say) 4,000*l*., and the Company had a large amount of valuable plate, which was ultimately (in part) turned into cash.

But the organisation[1] of the Guilds, and their connection with the Lord Mayor, must not be overlooked; if, therefore, they could be brought under any legal obligation to supply the Crown or Parliament with money, public finance would be greatly facilitated. The civic assessment was based on the supposed wealth of the individual members of each Guild, and the Merchant Taylors' Company had for some years stood at the head of the list, and bore one-tenth part of the total assessment.[2]

---

[1] As to this, see vol. 13 (2nd ser.), page 283, of Proc. Society Antiq., Life of Sir John Yorke, C. and M. T., Sheriff 1549.

[2] *j*, pages 33—59, 405. The assessments on all the Companies from 1548 to 1603 are printed, and see p. 329, note.

The subject came before the Grocers on October 7th, and they sent two of their members to interview the Lord Mayor, and to give him plainly to understand that if they advanced 4,500*l.*, the amount of their assessment, it was not to be construed into an engagement to furnish any part of the residue of the 200,000*l.* They obtained this assurance on the 10th, and then voted their 4,500*l.* The Merchant Taylors' Company made, as we shall see, no such condition.

Reynardson brought the matter before the Merchant Taylors on the 9th of October. These letters were laid before them, 1st, the King's sign manual letter, the last, as I think, that ever reached the Company from any of our Sovereigns; 2nd, the Peers' letter; 3rd, the Lord Mayor's letter; and "It was resolved, without debate, that the Company do provide the sum of 5,000*l.*, and the Master do call in all such money as is owing to the Company by bond, or otherwise;" the Peers' bond being given to Mr. Clement Mosse, for the Company (*b*), as he would be Master at the date fixed for the repayment of the loan.

Part of the loan was raised and the whole paid as under.
The part raised—

£	s.	d.	
516	5	0	from the Merchant Adventurers.
1,091	1	8	from the merchants trading to the East Indies.
1,908	10	0	from Captain Langham and six other liverymen.[1]

3,515 16 8

The whole was paid to the Exchequer, as to—

£
2,500 on the 22nd October⎫
2,000 on the 28th   ,, ⎬ On the Peers' bond,
500 on the 29th   ,, ⎭

the entries closing with these characteristic payments :—

"Item : paid for 2 dynners at Westminster, when the V^{m} £ was paid into the Exchequer, for the teller's foure officers and the Clerk of the Company xxxviijs."

---

[1] The Grocers raised 3,536*l.* from five persons, two only of whom were Grocers (The MS. Records of the Grocers' Company). The repayment was to be made to them in October, 1641, by the Company.

There is one name in this list of debtors we must not pass over without notice, viz., Captain Langham, one of those citizen soldiers who made up the Parliamentary Army. He was a Suffolk man, his father, Simon, being a clothier living at Bury St. Edmunds, and he was apprenticed on the 21st May, 1599, to Nicholas Smyth, of Thames Street. He became free by servitude in August, 1609, of the Livery in July, 1616, Warden in 1636 and 1637, then no doubt a prosperous man. He was useful to the Company, for when Sir R. Gurney asked them to strengthen Derry against the Irish rebels he was one of the Committee appointed in April, 1642, to expend 100 marks in the purchase of ordnance. When the Civil War began he had to go out into the field to hold one of the posts between London and Oxford. While there he was elected, on the 11th July, 1643, to be Master of the Company, and this is his letter of the 13th, pleading not only military duty, but, what was worse, a sickness shortly to be fatal, as grounds for exemption from serving without fine :—

"Great Brickhill, the 13 July, 1643.

"RIGHT WORSHIPFUL. Yours of the 11th of this present I have received, understanding thereby that you have been pleased to choose me Master of that Honble Compy for the year ensuing. I wish it lay in my power to do you service, and I would willingly accept of it. I fell sick upon Tuesday last of a fever, and receiving your letter this morning, I sent presently to his Excellency to ask leave to go to London for the recovery of my health and give you a verbal answer, but I thought I had satisfied you at my last being at London, but to submit myself to a fine I cannot, for the greater office gives way to the less. Nay, my Lord General would not give me leave to go to London, although as I am I am not able to serve the State nor your Worships. And therefore I pray you to choose such other able man for the place. And thus, praying you to excuse my scribbling lines, with my service remembered to our Master, Wardens, and Assistants, I end, and ever remain

"Your servant at command,
"GEORGE LANGHAM."

An order from the House of Commons is set out on the Court Minutes requiring his release from the service of the Company without fine, but that was needless, as death released him from all service on the 20th. This entry closes his career :—

" And then the Company being informed that Colonel George
Langham, lately elected Master of this Society for the year
ensuing, was departed this life, therefore the Company did proceed to the election of another fit person to be Master."

But to resume. Of course the 30th October was suffered to
pass without repayment of principal or any payment of interest,
but the debt was recognised by Parliament, for an ordinance was
passed on the 23rd of November, 1641, declaring that the loan
should be repaid out of such monies as should be raised by Parliament, and that for this purpose " an Act should be passed with
all expedition."[1] But none such was ever passed, as the last Act
to which Charles I gave his royal assent was that for the attainder
of Strafford,[2] which closes his reign of legislation.

Before we enter on the history of the second loan it may be
well to refer to the change that had come over the citizens in their
feelings towards the King, and the causes of it.

Upon Sir Henry Garraway's retirement, the King's party,
desiring to continue the line of Royalists, put Sir W. Acton in
nomination for the mayoralty. The election was then preceded by
Holy Communion and sermon, the manner of it the same as that
described by Fleetwood in Elizabeth's reign (*d*, pages 106—107 ;
j, page 21). The choice and nomination were with the Common
Hall,[3] and the selection was by the Court of Aldermen (*d*, page
115) of one of two sent to them from the electors. A Common
Hall[4] of young mechanics and other unqualified persons would
not hear of Acton,[5] for Soames and Wright had the most voices,

---

[1] This is set out in full (*b*, page 149).

[2] Charles I, c. 38.

[3] As to the history of this custom, see Stubbs' Constitutional History, vol. 3,
page 616.

[4] Appendix I.

[5] 1593, Sept. 7. William Acton, son of Richard Acton, Mercer, apprenticed to
     Thomas Henshawe, of Cheapside.

   1601, Jan. 18. Admitted to the freedom of Merchant Taylors' Company.

   1616, July 5. Admitted to Livery.

   1627, Feb. 29. An Assistant.

   1628, July 4. Received 33*l*. 6*s*. 8*d*. on election as Sheriff.

   Absent from the Court from 23rd Sept., 1640, till 7th April, 1641, and in this
     interval, viz., on 7th Oct., 1640, a deputation visited him to state
     that " the Court desired to preserve all good respect unto him, and to
     entreat his accustomed favour unto them." On the 29th Oct., 1642, he
     was one of 37 delinquents imprisoned by Parliament in Crosby House,
     Bishopsgate.—Cal. (D.S.), page 403.

   1650, Jan. 22. Died, having been present at the Court on 21st Oct. precedent.

but desired to be spared from serving. Acton was anxious only to know the King's mind, and resolved to hold office until the King should put him out. At a subsequent meeting, duly constituted, Acton was legally elected, but displaced by Parliament in favour of Wright.

The election of Sir R. Gurney,[1] the Royalist, was managed by the Sheriff of the King's party. "If London turn proselyte you need not doubt the general conversion," wrote Sir Peter Wroth to Mr. Secretary Vane (*d*, page 132); and he continues: "His election was [against the Puritans] abundantly victorious, because each party put themselves in battle array." It was not until Reynardson's election in 1648 that another Royalist held the civic chair.

To revert to general affairs. The Irish rebellion had led to the destruction of the Protestants of Ulster, and the King returned from Scotland to open Parliament and to take measures for its suppression. His arrival was during Sir Richard Gurney's[2] mayoralty (25th November, 1642), and he was received by him and the Corporation at Kingsland, upon his approach to London, and then entertained with great splendour at Guildhall. One incident of this reception may be noted, that the King, as a particular mark of affection to the City, gave back freely to them their Ulster estate, which, being in the hands of the rebels, was no great gift, as the King confessed; but he hoped to recover it first and then give it to the citizens whole and entire, adding "and for the legal part commandeth the Recorder to wait upon him to see it punctually performed" (*g*).

But the Parliament which had been assembled soon evinced a decided policy, not only against the King but against the Church, for the Presbyterians and Independents, who opposed each other upon every other, agreed upon one, subject, viz., to uproot the Church if possible. Episcopacy and Royalty thus became allied against these two common enemies.

The members for London in that Parliament were Thos. Soames,[3] the Grocer, Isaac Pennington,[4] the Fishmonger, Saml. Vassall, the Clothworker, and John Ven,[5] the Merchant Taylor.

---

[1] See his life in Dict. of N. B., vol. 20.
[2] Gurney was then knighted.
[3] Knighted 3rd Dec., 1641.
[4] Knighted by the Speaker in 1649, under Parliamentary Order (*d* 175); he was tried as a regicide but died before the execution of his sentence.
[5] It is spelt in the M.T.R. and C.J., in this way; on the King's warrant of execution as Venne.

Two of these, Pennington and Ven, were the decided enemies of the Church, of which it may be well to give an illustration. Persecution set in against the Clergy, and a conspicuous case was that of the Rev. Robert Chestlin,[1] the Rector of St. Matthew, Friday Street. His tithes were stopped, and when he summoned the defaulter before the Lord Mayor, Sir Edward Wright, under the City Tithe Act of Henry VIII, Pennington, though not a parishioner, attended the hearing, abused him by calling him " saucy Jock " and brazen-faced fellow, and other terms, yet, failed, after threatening the Lord Mayor, to get the case dismissed. Chestlin's persecution did not end here; subscriptions were got up to make a case against him. Failing in the House of Commons, they brought an accusation against him for a sermon preached on the 23rd October, 1642, obtained a warrant for his apprehension, riotously assaulted him in his own house, and carried him in great triumph before Pennington, then Lord Mayor, where Ven, as leader of the mob, stood forth accusing him as a seditious preacher and delinquent, and ultimately getting him sent to Colchester gaol, to remain there during the pleasure of the House.

As Ven will often come under our notice in this memoir, it may be well to give an outline of his life. He was the son of Simon Ven, of Liddeard St. Lawrence, Somersetshire, Yeoman; and as the apprentice of a Merchant Taylor, William Priestly, of Bread Street, became a freeman on the 27th August, 1610; and on the 2nd July, 1621, a liveryman, paying the sum of 35l. as his fine. His trade was a silk mercer in Cheapside, probably in St. Matthew's, Friday Street : he took a leading part as a mob orator for the Parliament (*d*, page 188). In 1641 he thought an appeal to the sword inevitable,[2] and he was one whom the King would have exempted from a general pardon.[3] He rose to be a Colonel of Horse in the Army of the West (393), and became in 1647, Governor of Windsor.[4] He was Warden (Renter) in 1641, and Senior in 1642, but excused as Master, as this Minute of 21st July, 1648, shows :—" Colonel Ven (*b*, page 294) appeared and excused himself from service as by an Ordinance of Parliament (to which he did submit when he left his service at Windsor Castle); he is exempt from all service save only that in Parliament, of which he is a member for London." He was one of the judges for

---

[1] Walker's Sufferings of the Clergy, part 2, page 166.
[2] 2 Clar., page 91.
[3] *Ibid.*, page 342.
[4] See indices to the collection of State Papers on date.

the trial of Charles I, and signed and sealed the warrant for his execution as John Venne (*k*, page 1053). He was reported to have hanged himself, or, at least, he died strangely and suddenly on the 28th June, 1650.[1]

The events following upon the assembly of this Parliament are part of the history of England, but happening in London, and as the citizens took a leading part in some of them, these must be briefly glanced at.

The King remained in London for some months, and having given the Commons a perpetual life, and otherwise done as much injury to his own cause as he well could do, he, under circumstances now to be adverted to, left London, never again to return until brought up for execution.

On the 1st January[2] the King went to the House of Commons to arrest Hampden and Pym[3] and three other members, but failed to do so, as, warned of his intentions, they fled to the City and took refuge in Coleman Street, the stronghold of the Puritans.[4] A panic seized upon the citizens, which was not lessened by the appearance of Charles at the Guildhall on the 5th, to demand the surrender of the five members, and afterwards as a voluntary guest to dine with Sir George Garrett, the Sheriff having no sympathy with his cause.[5] The City thus became the stronghold of the Parliamentary party, and the Commons resolved to appoint a Grand Committee to sit at " the Guildhall, possibly as a matter of personal security, at 3 P.M. to consider of our safety and the assistance of Ireland." Accordingly this Committee sat there on the 6th, and, after deliberation, declared the acts of the King to be a breach of privilege of their House, and this resolution was posted and circulated in the City the same night.

The excitement increased, for rumours were current that Coleman Street was to be attacked and that troops were to enter Ludgate between 9 and 10 of the same night; but the citizens were not wanting in energy to defend themselves, for such was the civic organisation, that in the space of an hour 40,000 men, with com-

---

[1] Heath's Chronicle, page 198; Smith's Obituary.

[2] The old style is used, the year ending in March.

[3] The Arrest of the Five Members, by John Forster, page 253.

[4] Amongst the principal inhabitants were Aldermen Pennington and Avery and Deputy Owen Rowe, Colonel of the 5th Regiment : they, with 10 other laymen, acted as a committee, " with Dr. Taylor, the Minister," to judge persons whether they be such as to be admitted to Holy Communion. See an interesting paper on the Parish Records, by Dr. Freshfield, in vol. 50, page 24, Archæ.

[5] The Arrest of the Five Members, by John Forster, pages 259, 330.

plete arms, and near 100,000 more with halberds, &c., were ready to act on the order of the Lord Mayor (Gurney).[1]

The Grand Committee, for more convenience of business, adjourned to the Grocers' Hall, sitting there on Friday and Saturday (the 7th and 8th). Sunday was a day of suspense, but 4,000 Bucks yeomen, ultimately raised to 6,000, equipped for the protection of John Hampden, appeared in London. As the capture of the five members ceased to be an apprehension, they appeared at the Grocers' Hall before the Committee on the third meeting (the 10th), and were taken in grand triumph to Westminster on the 11th, "there," writes Clarendon,[2] "the members being in this manner placed upon their thrones, the King retired with his poor family to Hampton Court."

So long as the members remained in the City, all the shops were shut, as if an enemy had been at their gates, but confidence rather in the Parliament than in the King was gradually regained, and, after this incident, Committees of the Commons sat from time to time in the halls of the Grocers', Merchant Taylors', and other Companies, for the despatch of public business.

The next controversy of vital importance[3] which we need notice was for the power of the sword. The King would not consent that Parliament should muster and array the militia, nor would they consent to his doing so, therefore the two Houses passed an Ordinance which placed the power in their own hands (*c*, pages 460—464 and 555). Out of this arose proceedings of impeachment (*k*, page 152) against two or three citizens. The offender first selected was George Benyon, a silkman, who deemed it to be his duty, as a freeman who had sworn to maintain the franchises and customs of London,[4] to petition the Commons against the Militia Ordinance, as depriving the Lord Mayor and Corporation of their undoubted right of supporting and commanding the City train bands. The course that he had taken in framing this petition had the approval of the Lord Mayor and Recorder, but this did not avail him, for he was disfranchised, fined in 3,000*l.*, and imprisoned in Colchester Castle. Then articles of impeachment were (5th July, 1642) filed against Sir R. Gurney as Lord Mayor (whom the extreme party were too anxious to depose) for publishing the King's proclamation for suppressing petitions to

---

[1] The Arrest of the Five Members, by John Forster, page 323.

[2] Vol 2, page 170.

[3] Neal's History of the Puritans, vol. 2, pages 469—170.

[4] The oath, &c., *j*, page 14.

Parliament, and for advising Benyon to petition, and lastly, for refusing to obey the two Houses in ordering him to assemble a Common Hall. Upon these charges he was dismissed from his mayoralty and sent to the Tower during the pleasure of the House. Sir Thomas Gardiner, the Recorder, had also articles presented against him which were not proceeded with.[1]

The Houses of Parliament then took measures of defence and for the suppression of the Irish revolt, acting as of necessity without the King's sanction. As wanting money, it might become a question how far the citizens, when applied to, would recognise their authority to pledge the credit of the kingdom and be disposed to assist them as borrowers and upon what security, when they presented themselves to them as such; therefore we will now trace the history of :—

II. The loan of 100,000*l.* in 1642 on the security of a Parliamentary Ordinance.

Public necessity having arisen, the City was again solicited for money. The Commons thereupon forthwith appointed a committee of two of their members, Ven (*c,* page 571) and Pennington, to consider and report as to the fittest way to call together the Livery Companies.

I do not find that they ever presented their report, but the Houses, in fact, adopted the same expedient which the King had found to be so successful in raising the first loan. They commanded the Lord Mayor to summon a Common Hall (*c, f*), on the 2nd June, at 4 P.M., and then appointed a deputation from each House to be present at it; Ven having to communicate this order to the Lord Mayor.

At the Common Hall—not, let it be noticed, the Common Council—Mr. Pym attended, and no doubt presented the case in the best aspect to the citizens. However, he was not altogether successful; he reported the result to the Commons in one way, and the Lord Mayor (Gurney) (*k,* pages 159—166; *f,* pages 1642—49), somewhat differently. According to Pym, the proposal for the loan was "received with great alacrity, and the citizens willingly condescended to it." According to the Lord Mayor, the money was to be raised by the Companies; each particular Company giving the security of its Seal to the members lending the money, but "that they desired to have an Ordinance

---

[1] See more as to Gardiner in Verney Family, London, 1892, vol. 1, page 334, and vol. 2, page 59, *et seq.*

passed for their security" (*c*, *f*) which was accordingly done before the subject was broached with the Companies.

This Ordinance of the 4th[1] described the loan as made "for one year, towards the preservation of Ireland" (in which then, as now, the Companies thought they owned land),[2] and the urgent affairs of the Kingdom; expressed the thanks of both Houses and of the whole Kingdom to the City, and declared that "the whole and every part of the loan should be duly repaid with 8*l.* per cent. out of the first and next moneys to be granted by Act of Parliament."

The Companies were now to be approached. The Commons seemed to think it expedient to have them summoned on different days (*c*, pages 606—608), as the Mercers, Grocers, Drapers, and Fishmongers, who could probably be relied upon, and would, by their decision, influence the others, on Tuesday the 7th, and the others, four on Wednesday (the 8th) and four on Thursday (the 9th); but, at any rate, that these meetings should not be held without some deputed member of the House being present. Accordingly, on the 4th (*c*, page 605), several members were appointed "to attend and urge the loan in the best way they could."

The Grocers met on the 7th, and, as the name of Soames[3] was well known and respected, he attended as a deputation: was successful in obtaining their sanction to the loan, and, on reporting this, had the thanks of the House of Commons (*c*, page 612). The entry in the Grocers' records of this meeting is thus prefaced :—" After reading, &c., in the presence of divers right worshipful persons of the Commons House of Parliament, it pleased them to entreat and persuade the Company to perform the contents of the said Ordinance, showing the necessity thereof, and giving confident assurance, not only for the repayment of the moneys now to be lent, but also of the former moneys lent by this Company upon the security of divers Lords, it was, with a general vote and consent, agreed that the said loan of 9,000*l.* should be lent towards the defence and relief of the distressed Kingdom of Ireland."

The Grocers raised this loan by voluntary subscriptions amongst their own members; each Alderman being pleased to subscribe 500*l.*, and each of the Assistants, Livery, and Yeomanry adding his name in the book of subscriptions. Baron Heath "could not

---

[1] *b*, Report on the Irish Society, 1891, May 4, page 222.

[2] *Ibid.*

[3] The M.P. for London and the son of Sir Stephen, Lord Mayor in 1598, and of the Grocers' Company.

discover the reason why the enormous sum of 9,000*l.* had been assessed on the Company," and, possibly was ignorant of the corn assessment then in force, which was the basis of this loan.[1]

The Lord Mayor's precept was sent to the Merchant Taylors' Company on the 4th. It stated that the Livery assembled in the Common Hall had freely agreed that 100,000*l.* should be forthwith furnished by the several Livery Companies ; and, therefore, his order was that the Master and Wardens should, with all convenient speed, raise the sum of 10,000*l.* according to the existing corn assessment.

The Master for the year was a very competent man (Clement Mosse) who had been many years the Clerk (*i*, page 81), and was well versed in the law and traditions of the Company ; he presided at the Hall on the 10th, where the whole Company,[2] including the Livery and Bachelors, were assembled to take the precept into consideration. Captain Ven attended the meeting as a deputation from the Commons. To the Merchant Taylors it seemed that the question of primary importance was this : Had the Lord Mayor any legal authority for issuing his precept, *i.e.*, his order, or, in other words, could the Common Hall lawfully determine that the Master and Wardens should raise this sum by assessment ? That it was not in accordance with precedent was clearly shown to the Company ; thus :—

"And then our Master acquainted the said assembly with former precedents in what manner moneys desired to be borrowed of this Company were furnished.

"*Precedents of Crown Loans.*

"One, of the sum of 1,100*l.*, lent unto Queen Elizabeth in Anno 1598, of the Assistants, Livery, and Members of the Bachelors of this Company proportionably towards the loan of 20,000*l.*, which was repaid in Anno 1599. Another of 1,350*l.*, lent to King James in Anno 1604 by the Assistants, Livery, and Bachelors of this Company towards the loan of 15,000*l.*, which was repaid in 1607 ; and another sum of 6,000*l.*, raised upon the Assistants and Livery of this Society, Anno Dom. 1627, in the 3rd year of our Sovereign Lord King Charles, towards the loan of 60,000*l.*, which was likewise repaid with interest the same year. Which several precedents were openly read, being registered in the books of this Company,

---

[1] *History*, page 111.
[2] *b*, page 184. Mr. Essex, of the Merchant Taylors' Hall, has made these extracts for me.

together with the names of the particular lenders in the said loans."

There was no case in which such a precept had ever been sent to the Company, and to accept its authority would be fraught with grave evil. For it would take the property of the Livery Company out of the control of the Master and Wardens, and place it at the mercy of a popular assembly, acting without either authority or responsibility.

The meeting, therefore, came to this resolution :—

" That the Common Hall (consisting of the Liveries of this city) assembled in the Guildhall, London, hath no power, right, or authority to bind or impose upon this Company any loan of money whatsoever, and what they did in the said Common Hall was of no validity or force to compel this Company to lend or part with any money or other thing, but that this loan was, and ought to be, voluntary, without enforcement at all; yet, nevertheless, the Company of themselves were very willing and forward (as much as in them lay) to set forward and furnish the said 10,000*l.* so desired to be lent."

However, as the money might have to be raised by voluntary loan, to whom should the individual members lend it ? To Parliament or to the Company ? But, first, could not the Master and Wardens call in the money lent to the Crown on the Peers' Bond, as they had called in the money due to them from their fellow citizens last year ? Would not the Ordinance of October, 1641, entitle them to payment ? Captain Ven was therefore requested to secure the immediate repayment of the loan of 5,000*l.*, out of the 400,000*l.* which the two Houses had authorised to be raised ; but all that he could do " was to promise his best endeavours therein."

It was certain that all the stock of the Company was exhausted, including, unfortunately, " their trust moneys to be used for good and charitable uses." If, therefore, money had to be borrowed, what security should be offered to the lenders ? The minute thus proceeds : " And then our Master propounded two ways which he conceived to be the best for raising of 10,000*l.*, the one by the particular loan of such as would rely upon the security of the Ordinance of Parliament, the other by the credit of the Common Seal of this Society, to be given to such persons and members of this Company who would lend upon the same, declaring unto them that if the Company should be at a loss therein, the particular members of the said Company ought to make the same good to the desires of benefactors who intrusted this Company therewith. And although our Master inclined to the former of the two propositions, alleging that he had rather lose such part of his own than the Company's moneys, yet it was agreed that it should be put to the question whether of the two ways last expounded should be put in practice for the levying of the said 10,000*l*. And it was fully and unanimously agreed upon the question that the said 10,000*l*. shall be forthwith taken up and furnished upon the credit of the Common Seal of this Society. And for that this Company is desirous to have the same rather furnished by the brethren and members thereof than otherwise, this Company is contented to allow to every lender interest or forbearance thereof after the rate of 8*l*. per cent. per annum, and to give their Common Seal for repayment thereof accordingly."

In order to provide against the eventuality of non-payment by Parliament within the year, and the urgent necessity of those now lending to the Company, the members who were assembled gave this authority to the Master and Wardens:—

" If the sum of 10,000*l*. shall not be repaid to the Company within one year, every lender shall receive from the Master interest at the rate of 8*l*. per cent. per annum. And it is further ordered and resolved upon for the better and more speedy satisfaction of them (if occasion shall require, which God forbid) to make sale of the Company's lands, plate, and goods, and by such other means as shall be held most fitting, whereby no partie in this loan shall sustain any loss by this Company."

But this meeting was not final, for though matters were urgent and Parliament had issued an order on the 10th for plate to be brought into the Guildhall as bullion (*f*, page 1312), and as on the 11th the Commons had sent a deputation into the City to thank the citizens for their loan and so to hasten its payment, yet the Merchant Taylors did not arrange for their advance until they had met on the 15th (*b*) and ordered their Clerk "to examine the Ordinance of Parliament, tendered as security for the 10,000*l*., and perfect the date and do such other things thereabout as shall be required," and decided that the bonds to be given to the several lenders should be sealed with the Common Seal of the Society in the presence of the Wardens (*b*, page 151).

The money was raised in two subscriptions and paid in seven instalments from June 20th to August 22nd. First, 7,000*l*. was advanced to the Company by 40 of its members in various sums, and 3,000*l*. by eight members. Reynardson, who was present at both Courts, advanced 500*l.* for the first, and 2,400*l.* for the second instalment.

This, like the other loan, was the occasion of some sumptuary expenses, thus : " Item paid and spent at dinners when Mr. Bayley (who was Clerk to the Bachelors' Company) and some others divers days attended at the Hall, at the receipt and payment of the 10,000*l.* and at other times . . . 3*l.*"

Mention has been made of the notice of the 10th of June issued by Parliament for plate to be brought into the Guildhall. The money so raised was to furnish and maintain an army " for the defence of the King and Parliament."[1] The loans were described as a good and acceptable service to the Commonwealth, and a promise was made to repay the lenders at 8 per cent. interest. As a counterblast, the King wrote to the Lord Mayor that if the citizens advanced any money upon these votes, he should look at it as raising a force against himself ; and he issued a notice inviting his subjects to bring in their plate to him at York.

The enthusiasm of the people for the Parliamentary cause was soon evidenced, according to Echard ; as within 10 days so vast a proportion of plate was brought in, that there were hardly men enough to receive, or room to store, it ; the citizens did not only bring in their best plate, but their wives delivered up their candle cups and rings, even their thimbles and bodkins to maintain the " good old cause."[2] The total so raised in London, Middlesex, and Essex amounted, according to his authority, to 11,000,000*l.*, and though this amount is qualified by Neal[3] and reduced to 1,267,326*l.*, it contrasts strangely with the difficulty of raising money on loan from Livery Companies.[4]

III. The loan of 50,000*l.* to the Corporation of London in 1643.[5]

I do not trace on the Corporation Records or the Commons' Journals any report from Ven as to the meeting of the Merchant

---

[1] This order is printed verbatim, and the subsequent letter and proclamation of the King, 14th June, in Rush., vol. 2, page 743.

[2] Echard, vol. 2, page 320.

[3] History of the Puritans, vol. 2, page 487. Clarendon says the sums so raised amounted to incredible proportions (vol. 3, page 363).

[4] I can find nothing in the Calendar of State Papers to confirm either of these statements. The total value of the plate in the Tower of London, taken at 5s. or 5s. 4d. per oz., in August, 1649, was 14,221*l.* 15s. 4d. (vol. 15, Archæ., page 290).

[5] The Lord Mayor (Pennington) on June 30th, 1643, sent books to the several Livery Companies for subscriptions to be given for the relief of Ireland (vol. 9, page 171).

Taylors, or the protest which they made against the use of the
Lord Mayor's precepts for raising loans from the Livery Companies
by the Common Hall; but, as Reynardson was a member of the
Corporation and Ven of the Commons, the fact of such a protest
may have been made known to these assemblies. However, it
was not again resorted to in raising this third loan, although the
ostensible purpose for which it was raised, viz., the defence of the
City, might have afforded some justification for its use ; but
before entering upon its history, some mention must be made of
events happening in the City.

War between the King and Parliament was in effect declared by
Essex being appointed to command the Parliamentary forces in July
and the King having set up his standard at Nottingham in August,
1642. Shortly after, Sir R. Gurney was, as we have seen, displaced as Lord Mayor when Sir George Whitmore, the Haber-
dasher and the Lord Mayor of 1631, was ordered to summon the
Common Hall for the appointment of a successor, when Isaac Pennington was chosen and elected.

In November Prince Rupert took possession of Brentford, but his
forces were dispersed by 24,000 men of the train bands[1] who were
dispatched from London. It became necessary for Parliament to
raise money to bear these army expenses, and as 30,000*l.* was
wanted, Pennington on the 26th put forth a manifesto to be read
in all churches on the next Sunday (the 27th), upon which the
several ministers were to stir up the parishioners, the churchwardens after the service were to assemble them and raise a
proportionate part of this fund—to be paid to the Guildhall on the
next Tuesday (*g*, pages 71—73).

But this was not enough, as the burthen must be borne not by
the willing but by all citizens, therefore the two Houses passed an
Ordinance on the 29th November, stating in the preamble that the
King would not give his Royal assent, but authorising Pennington
and seven other Aldermen,[2] or any four of them, to assess those in
their wards who had not voluntarily contributed, such assessment
not to exceed the twentieth part of their estate, and this taxation
was extended over the whole of England on the 8th December.
As the estimated annual cost of the Army was 1,000,000*l.* and of the
Navy 300,000*l.*, on the 24th February commissioners were named
in each county for assessing the tax on the residents therein, a

---

[1] G. G. R., page 66.
[2] Martin, Towse, Warner, Andrews, Chambers, Fowke, and Somers.

taxation estimated to produce 1,600,000*l.* at the rate of 5*l.* per man as an assessment.[1]

In May, 1643, two citizens were brought before a court-martial upon a charge of conspiracy to aid the King within the bills of mortality, by seizing the Lord Mayor, all the outworks to the City, recently ordered (*c*, 7th March), and resisting all the payments levied by Parliament. Sir Nicholas Crispe's Commission of Array of March, 1643, was brought to the notice of the Court, but they were both condemned; and one, Chaloner, an eminent citizen living in Cornhill, was gibbeted opposite to his own doorway. His confession, or speech on the scaffold, is worthy of notice as expressing no sadness or contrition for the King's cause having failed, but his conviction "that he was a great deal in fault in having engaged in such an enterprize against the Parliament."[2]

The King's forces were alleged to be advancing towards London, and the Common Council (*a*) on the 18th July (Reynardson not being present) met and resolved as follows :—

"At this Common Council intelligence was received from the House of Commons that divers troops of the King's horse were come nigh unto this city, and that there were great risings of ill-affected people in Kent and Surrey. And this court duly weighing and considering the great and imminent danger this city is in, and the urgent need of the speedy raising of money to be employed in the defence thereof, ordained that money should be borrowed on the credit of the common seal at the rate of 8*l.* per cent.[3]

But on August 1st[4] they altered this resolution by determining that the money should be raised in wards, and that a Parliamentary Ordinance should be obtained for the assessment of all persons within the command of the forts or lines of communication.

The City really wanted peace, and petitions for it were presented to both Houses on the 5th (*e*, page 199; *f*, page 160)

---

[1] Clarendon, vol. 3, page 369. An assessment of 1,418,299*l.* for the year ending 30th June, 1644, yielded only 260,306*l.* 14*s.* 5*d.*

[2] *k*, page 634, and 4 Clar. Reb., page 63.

[3] Present (18th July)—

T. Pennington (Mayor).

Aldermen		
Thomas Aitkin.		Samuel Warner.
Sir T. Wollaston.		Thomas Foot.
J. Warner.		John Kendrick.
J. Fowke.		
James Bunce.		John Langham } Sheriffs.
Wm. Gibbs.		Thomas Andrews }

[4] 15 Aldermen, including the Sheriffs, were present.

(the women of London presenting a similar petition on the 9th); but this policy ill suited Pennington. Between him and the King the struggle was one of life or death, for the King had excepted him from any general pardon (*f*, page 158), believing that he had discerned in him and in Ven the intention, which they afterwards fulfilled, of taking away his life.[1] Accordingly Pennington called a meeting of the Common Council for the evening of Sunday, the 6th of August,[2] to petition both Houses against peace accommodations with the King, which petition was presented to the Commons on the 7th (*c*, page 197), having attached to it a draft Ordinance, which the petitioners desired should be passed forthwith to authorise a loan.

If Pennington's party was to be aided vigorous measures were needed, and if money was to be raised for immediate use some more expeditious method of raising it must be adopted than the taxation of wardsmen. Therefore, on the 11th, having got the Tower of London handed over to the citizens (*c*, p. 201), he obtained a resolution from the Common Council (*a*) to raise the money from the Livery Companies, such a loan to be ultimately confirmed by Parliamentary Ordinance (*c*, page 209).

On the 16th (*b*) a letter was submitted, from the Lord Mayor, to Reynardson and his colleagues of the Merchant Taylors' Company, stating that, as the City was in imminent danger by reason of the near approach of the King's forces, he and his brethren the Aldermen had resolved that the sum of 50,000*l*. should be forthwith lent by the several Companies upon the common seal of the City, to be repaid in six months' time with interest at 8*l*. per cent. per annum, and "praying the Company to contribute 5,000*l*. towards the said loan, to pay the same to the Treasurers for plate and money at the Guildhall."

Ven, who in March had obtained out of the last loan the payment of 2,277*l*. (*d*, page 448) for his regiment of horse, was not

---

[1] *g*, vol. 5, p. 111. King's reply given at Oxford to the City, Jan., 1642 (Clar. Reb., vol. 3, page 618).

[2] Present (August 6, 1643) —

T. Pennington, Mayor.

Aldermen		
	Thos. Aitkin.	Wm. Gibbs.
	Sir T. Wollaston.	Rich. Chambers.
	John Warner.	Sam. Warner.
	John Towse.	Wm. Barkley.
	John Fowke.	Wm. Ashwell.
	James Bunce.	John Langham } Aldermen and
		Thos. Andrews } Sheriffs.

present to urge Pennington's proposal; and as the preceding loans, though lent on what was then deemed to be good security, remained unpaid, the Court resolved :—"To refer the same to a more ample Court (15 members being present) to conclude thereupon;" a course which contrasts strangely with that adopted by the Grocers' Company, who, on the same day, resolved unanimously that the 4,500*l.*," their share of the loan, "should be forthwith taken up on the Company's security, and lent to the City upon the general seal thereof" (*bb*); and on the 7th of September resolved "that the remainder of their plate (reserving so much thereof as shall amount to the value of 300*l.* for necessary use and service), be forthwith sold and disposed of to make up the 4,500*l.* agreed to be lent " (*bb*).

But there were reasons for caution, as the Merchant Taylors might have looked upon Pennington's letter[1] as a political stratagem, and as committing them to a more decided line of action against the King than they were disposed to adopt. True, the King's party in the Company might be on the wane; for though the Company feasted themselves on Charles'[2] return from Scotland, on the 25th November, 1641, yet the dinner in commemoration of the "Coronation," an annual festival up to March, 1641,[3] had since been abandoned. Then, again, this money, though asked for the protection of London, might, in fact, be used for other purposes. That such a suspicion was present with them in May is evident, for when they gave out the arms of the Company to the Lord Mayor, who had authority to require them under the Act of the Common Council, of 27th April, they added this condition " that they should be used *only* for the defence of the City,"[4] and their suspicion would be strongly confirmed by a letter from Weavers' Hall, read at the Court on the 22nd August, stating "the urgent necessities for the relief of Gloucester," and praying the "payment of the loan to the treasurers of plate and money, at the Guildhall, without delay."[5] Reynardson, with only 10 others, was present at this Court (*b*, page 181), and, in consequence of this small attendance, the subject was again adjourned, and the whole Company (Assistants and Bachelors) were summoned for the 25th, when the meeting was again adjourned.

---

[1] Remembrancia, page 201.

[2] Paid for dinners of the Court and Livery, 29*l.* 16*s.*—*b*.

[3] Paid stewards, 6*l.* 13*s.* 4*d.*—*b*, page 143.

[4] As to these arms see *i*, page 554. A claim was made by the Company on March 15, 1650, for 120*l.* as their value, as they were never returned.—*b*, page 164.

[5] *Ibid.*, page 181.

Thus to act was trifling with the subject, and, therefore, on the 28th, two meetings were held at which Reynardson was present; the first, in the Court Room, of Assistants to increase their number by adding six new Assistants,[1] and "then in the Hall," of the Livery Warden Substitutes and 16 men, with divers of the Bachelors, to whom these questions were put and answered in the affirmative. (1) That the 5,000*l.* should be raised. (2) That the Common Seal should be given to such persons as should lend the same. (3) That so much of the plate as could be conveniently spared should be sold; and, lastly, it was "unanimously agreed and consented to that authority should be given to the Master and Wardens to sell so much of the Company's goods and lands to make good the loan in case—[which was the event which happened]—it shall not be repaid to the Company" (*b*, page 1827).

The money raised amounted by loan to 5,200*l.*, and by the sale of plate to 889*l.*,[2] but only 4,050*l.*, was paid to the Guildhall, and this in 13 instalments, from the 2nd of September, 1643, to the 20th of May following. Those who lent the Company money were 26 in number, some not being members and residing in the country. Reynardson advanced only 100*l.*; Sir Henry Pratt, 250*l.*,[3] and later another 250*l.*; Clement Mosse, originally, 200*l.*, and then another 100*l.*; Thomas Juxon, 100*l.*[4]; Lady Melton, a non-member, 200*l.*: sums which probably evinced the political feeling of the lenders, for Sir W. Acton, Bart., neither attended the meetings nor made any advance of money.

---

[1] The reasons assigned in the resolution were:—"(1) Divers Assistants are for the most part out of town, many of whom seldom come to the Hall; and (2) Some absent themselves, whereby the businesses of the Company are like to suffer." Four of the six were sworn in at the Court of November 10th, when Reynardson and 15 other members were present.

[2] The purchasers were: Viner, 875*l.* 19*s.* 8*d.*; Pratt, 8*l.* 6*s.* 8*d.*; Bardolph, 4*l.* 14*s.* 8*d.*

[3] Sir Henry Pratt, Bart., the son of Henry Pratt, of Cirencester, Clothier, was apprenticed to Anthony Baker, December 8, 1587, and made free on November 24, 1595, by Reginald Walters, who had married the wife and executrix of Anthony Baker. He was admitted to the Livery July 16, 1610; elected Third or Upper Renter Warden, July 17, 1627; elected Second Warden July 13, 1630; elected Master August 4. He was elected Alderman for Bridge Ward February, 1630, and Sheriff in 1631, but never Lord Mayor. In March, 1640, his ward was vacant and George Clarke, the Grocer, elected to it. He was knighted and made a baronet at Windsor July 26, 1646.

[4] A relative of Dr. Juxon, the Archbishop, who was educated at the Merchant Taylors' School. A Scholarship is still existing for St. John's, Oxford, under the will of John Juxon of August 17, 1626.

Such, in outline, is the history of the three loans made by the Livery Companies, and it would be incomplete if we did not add that they have never been repaid, except as hereafter appears, either by the Crown or Parliament, or the Corporation of London. The creditors of the Merchant Taylors' Company lost nothing, as the goods and estates of the latter were sold to repay the loans when they were called for.

As to the first loan, these payments were made by Gilbert Harrison, the City Chamberlain. In 1644-45, 500*l.*, and a like sum of 500*l.* in 1645-46, and at some later period 250*l.*, which would liquidate interest at 8*l.* per cent. and some part of the principal. The second and third loans were, as we shall see, otherwise dealt with.

In 1649 the Parliament confiscated the lands of the Deans and Chapters, and thereby the Mora Estate, in Finsbury, of which the Company had been lessees since November, 1556, the leases having been renewed ; the one then existing was granted to the Company in 1614 by Dr. Thomas White, the then Prebend of the Moor and afterwards the founder of Sion College. The Act, however, protected the leasehold interests.

The Company sought to acquire the fee simple from the Parliamentary Commissioners sitting at Gurney House[1] by "doubling," and on the 28th August authorised the Master and Wardens[2] to treat with them accordingly. The estate was valued at 600*l.*, and part of the third loan—that is 300*l.*—was taken as half the purchase money, the Company doubling, that is adding 300*l.* as the other half. This method of "doubling" was a device of the Parliament to cancel old debts and to obtain more money.[3]

As to the second and third loans, some attempt was made on the 15th March, 1650, with the Council of State for a settlement. As to the second, 1,000*l.* was deducted as the value of the Irish lands which had been restored to the Company, but no money was ever repaid for the 10,000*l.* advanced. As to the third, a balance of 2,843*l.* 4*s.* 10*d.* and interest was due after deducting 756*l.* 15*s.* 2*d.* as paid, 150*l.* assigned to St. John's, Oxford, and 300*l.*, "doubled at Gurney House," on 2nd October, 1649, in payment to the Dean and Canons of St. Paul's for the Mora Estate, Finsbury. A claim was also put forward by the Com-

---

[1] If the house of Sir R. Gurney, it was situated in the Old Jewry.
[2] (*i*), page 557.
[3] Preface to Cal. S. P., Advances of Money, page 7. The Acts encouraged doubling *c*, 24, Scoball, pages 16—22.

D

pany for 132*l.*, three-fifths of 220*l.* lent on the 11th March, 1643, as part of an assessment of 10,000*l.*, in respect of which the Companies were to be repaid at the rate of 24,000*l.* for each 40,000*l.* advanced (*b*, page 428).

These loans probably enhanced the importance of the Livery Companies as political factors in the struggle then raging. In June, 1642 (*g*), while the second loan was in negotiation, the King desired to address them through the Lord Mayor, but the Houses placed their interdict upon it. Again, in 1642, after Charles had withdrawn to Oxford, the City remonstrated (*g*, vol. 5, page 110), and sent a deputation of Aldermen and Common Council to present their petition to the King. A written reply was given to them; and that this might be widely known, the King wrote to the Sheriffs on the 17th January (*f*, vol. 3, page 49), requiring them " to take care for the publication, and directing that the Masters and Wardens of the several Livery Companies should forthwith summon ' all their members,' with all Freemen and Apprentices (whose hopes and interests are so much blasted by these distractions) belonging thereunto, to appear at their several Halls, where the Master and Wardens were to cause His Majesty's reply, together with his present letter, to be publicly read."

The Sheriffs, however, submitted this letter to Parliament, who forthwith ordered " that the several Companies should not assemble in their Halls for reading the reply, and the Lord Mayor and Sheriffs were desired to take special care to prevent the same " (*e*, vol. 2, page 941 ; *g*, vol. 5, page 122). The Houses made a direct communication to the Merchant Taylors' Company,[1] and, as there is no entry of the King's reply having been read either to the Company or to the Apprentices, the Parliamentary order was probably obeyed, but whether the like obedience was observed by the other Companies is doubtful, for Rushworth states that certain Masters and Wardens who had counselled the King in this matter were ordered into custody. At any rate, the Master and Wardens of the Grocers' Company, and their Clerk (Mr. Bunbury), were summoned to appear before a Committee of the House on 27th of

---

[1] 1642-43.—Item, paid to Stam's messengers from the Parliament to the Master and Wardens concerning the letters sent by the King's Majesty to them, 20*s.* ; spent by water to and from Westminster several times, and otherwise for potations for them in their attendance, 10*s.* ; and given at the Parliament House, 6*s.* ; and for coppies of the letters, order, and ticketts, 10*s.* ; *in toto*   } 2*l.* 6*s.*

January, and the Lord Mayor (Gurney) also appeared before the whole House on the 28th, to clear himself of the high charge laid against him in His Majesty's letter (*c*). Thus closed, so far as I know, all attempts by the Sovereign at direct communication with the Companies.

During the struggle against the King, Parliament, to advance their cause, never failed, as before observed, to make any use they pleased of the Halls of the several Companies, and one instance may have a special interest to readers of the Merchant Taylors' Company. The occasion was in January, 1643, when a dinner (of which I can trace no entry in the Commons' Journals or the records of the Merchant Taylors' Company) was given to the Lords and Commons,[1] nominally by the City, but in fact by the people, as it was paid for out of the subsidy money. It was to commemorate Brookes' plot, and to cement the City and the Houses in their contest against the King. The invited guests met at Christ Church, Newgate Street, to hear a sermon from Stephen Marshall,[2] "The Trumpet of the Long Parliament,"[3] and afterwards to proceed with civic state to the Hall. As they passed down Cheapside popish pictures and relics, placed on a scaffold where the cross formerly stood, were burnt before them.[4] Not an item of cost can be traced as having been incurred by the Merchant Taylors, nor indeed that any permission for the use of the Hall was asked.

"One thing is also very remarkable," wrote a contemporary critic, "that after they had been very honourably entertained at Merchant Taylors' Hall, and dinner ended, instead of idle maskings and other such unseemly actions heretofore used at such public meetings, to declare their union of spirit as in the presence of God all sang together the 67th Psalm to testify their thankfulness to God ; a religious precedent worthy to be imitated by all Christians in their public meetings."[5]

---

[1] January 3rd. The treasurers of the subsidy to pay the cost of the entertainment.—*a.*

[2] Sermon on January 18th, 1643. Printed by Boutell, 1644.

[3] Fuller adds : " In their sickness he was their confessor, in their assembly their counsellor, in their treaties their chaplain, and in their disputations their champion." He was of Emmanuel College, Cambridge ; died in 1655 ; and lies buried at Westminster."—Stanley's *Westminster Abbey*, page 224, note.

[4] *h* ; Gardiner, G. R., vol. 1, page 121 ; Camden Society, Miscellaneous, vol. 8. The cross stood opposite Wood Street, and had been pulled down during Pennington's mayoralty, on the 2nd May preceding.

[5] Extract from the *True Informer*, London.—Bates, 1643, No. 18, page 155. After Naseby a similar entertainment was given in Grocers' Hall, June 19, 1645, when the 46th Psalm was sung.

When the entertainment was given the Hall was surrounded with beautiful tapestries, called by the Puritans "offensive and superstitious pictures," which, in July, 1643, had been complained of to the Company, and shortly after this entertainment the Court ordered that the Wardens and six others of the Court should meet together and consider "of the charge of defacing of superstitious pictures in the hangings for the upper end of the Hall," which defacement was carried out, and in such condition they remained until removed from the Hall and sold for 20*l.* in 1720 (*i*, page 37, notes).

During the first war with the Parliament, which terminated in January, 1647, by the surrender of the King to the Parliamentary Commissioners at Newcastle, there can be little doubt by the following items in the Merchant Taylors' Accounts that they were in full sympathy with the success of the Parliamentary forces, thus:—

		£	s.	d.
1643–4.	Paid for seats at Paul's at thanksgiving service for York	£2	0	0
	„ for a dinner at the Hall on the 18th July, the day of the public thanksgiving for the deliverance at York	15	12	0
1644–5.	„ for a Thanksgiving Dinner on the 22nd July, 1645	20	2	6
1645–6.	„ for the Thanksgiving Dinner for Dartmouth	16	15	6
	„ to vergers of Paul's at the thanksgiving for Oxford	0	5	0
1646–7.	„ for a dinner, being several thanksgivings for the surrender of sundry towns and castles	6	13	4
1647–8.	„ for two Thanksgiving Dinners, one for Ireland, and one for several victories	0	12	6

With these dinners we may contrast the order of Parliament[1] to forbear one meal in a week, the value of which was to be devoted to supplying armed men.

But now to pursue the minor incidents of Reynardson's life. In 1645 some differences arose between him and his colleagues upon the vote of the Court on the 11th March, either political, in regard to paying the charges of the Thanksgiving Dinner for the taking of Chester from the King, or personal, in regard to the extension of the lease which he held from the Company, on which he had spent 300*l.*; which may account for his absence in November, 1646, when the presence of the wealthier members of the Company would be needed. It was the courtesy of this and earlier times for the citizens to welcome the arrival of foreign visitors

---

[1] *f*, March 20, 1643–44, page 242, and the entries in *a*, March and April.

or Ambassadors upon their disembarkation at the Tower Wharf.[1] Thus Prince Cassimer was so received in May, 1578, when he came to visit Sir Thomas Gresham in Bishopsgate Street. The Merchant Taylors appointed 32 of their members " in cotes of velvet, with chaynes of gold, on horseback, and every one of them having a man on horseback to attend him " (*j*, page 251), to receive the Prince. So now the Russian Ambassador was about to land at the Tower Wharf, and, that nothing might be wanting towards his entertainment, the Merchant Taylors were ordered by the Lord Mayor's Precept " to receive him in such manner as is usual to persons of like quality," and appointed six persons of the Company, with velvet cassocks and gold-chains, well mounted on horseback, to receive him at the wharf, and from thence to attend upon the Ambassador to his place of residence (*l*, page 535).

Reynardson, however, was not one of these six members, and he absented himself from the Hall until July 15th, 1647, the Court having in the meantime sent a deputation to him on June 23rd (*b*), to state " that his absence from the Court," and what was possibly then of more importance, " from other public meetings of this Company," where his counsel and assistance had been wanted, had been noticed, and entreating him, after mistake, if any on their part, had been put right, " to continue his good affection to this Company." After this his attendance continued to be regularly given until the 28th August, 1648, besides being an auditor of the Company's accounts for three years prior to 1647–48, when his mayoralty was approaching.

Hitherto we have found little to indicate the political party to which Reynardson was allied, and it is only his decided action as a Royalist in the office of Lord Mayor that gives us a clue to the principles which then, and possibly throughout his previous career, influenced him. The mayoralty was one of absolute selection by the citizens, and the character of the man chosen afforded some indication of the popular or political feeling then influencing them.

The two Lord Mayors before him were Sir John Gayre (the Presbyterian), 1646–47, and Warner (the Independent), 1647–48. The City was tired of the confusion, and the Apprentices on the

---

13th July, 1647,[1] petitioned for the King's restoration; towards the close of Gayre's mayoralty the citizens came into controversy with Parliament on the subject of a Militia Ordinance of the 23rd of July, as infringing upon their rights and privileges by substituting a Militia Committee selected by the army in displacement of that existing under the Ordinance of the 4th May, which the Corporation had selected, and was favourable to the King. Two petitions[2] were forthwith addressed to the Lord Mayor: one from "divers well affected," citizens, and the other from "divers young men, apprentices," and sent in to the House of Commons with a covering petition from the Common Council. These petitions were presented on the 24th, but both Houses had risen. The scenes of riot which ensued on Monday, the 26th, are thus reported by Rushworth[3] to Fairfax: at the sitting of the Lords the rioters broke into the House, and obliged them to pass a vote recalling the Ordinance. Then about 2 P.M. they went to the Commons, ultimately broke into their House, and towards 8 o'clock the sitting members also revoked the Ordinance. The Speaker left the chair, but was compelled to resume it that the House might pass a vote that the King should be presently brought to London.

During these riots the Lord Mayor and Civic Authorities were appealed to for, but failed to send, protection to the Houses. Fairfax therefore intervened on behalf of the army, and a correspondence ensued, which ended in the submission of the City. The army advanced to Southwark at 2 o'clock A.M. on the 5th August, and on the 6th took possession of the Tower (*l*, page 176).

An enquiry was then opened as to those who, as the Commons deemed, had acted tumultuously against them; and the result was an impeachment prepared on the 25th of September against the Lord Mayor Gayre, and a Common Hall was ordered to be held on the 28th for choosing his successor.[4] Riot was anticipated,

---

[1] The details of the Negotiations are given in the Vindication of the City, printed April 30, 1660 (James Flesher, London).—*e*, pages 202—206.

[2] These are set out in Rushworth, vols. 6 and 7, and 4 State Trials, page 959. Prints of them will also be found in the Guildhall Library.

[3] Fairfax Correspondence, vol. 1, pages 379—384.

[4] The Common Hall, September 28, 1647, held by Pennington. There were also present :—

	Aldermen		
Aldermen	Sir John Wollaston.	T. Andrews.	
	A. Reynardson.	R. Chambers.	
	J. Fowke.	John Kendrick.	
	Thos. Foot.	Thos. Viner.	
	George Williams.	Saml. Avery }	Aldermen and
	Thomas Atkin.	John Bide }	Sheriffs.

and a Lord Mayor's precept was issued for constables to appear with a strong body of householders in the Guildhall, during the election (*a*). Five Aldermen were first put in nomination : Warner, Andrews, Garrett, Soames, and Reynardson ; and then two only, Warner and Garrett, the former being chosen and sworn in at the Exchequer for the residue of Gayre's year, 1647–48.[1]

Of Warner's colleagues in the mayoralty, there is one whom we cannot pass over without notice, that is Richard Browne, the Sheriff, who was then a Woolmonger, but afterwards to become a Merchant Taylor, and as such the Lord Mayor of London, in succession to Reynardson, in 1660. Up to the date of his election as Sheriff he had been a distinguished leader of the Parliamentary forces throughout the first war with Charles. He served under Waller, and was the first to enter the breach at Winchester. He then shared the command at the victory of Alresford, and was constituted a Major-General for the reduction of Oxford. At the conclusion of the war he was appointed one of the Commissioners to receive the King from the Scots, and, being brought into contact with Charles at Holmby, is said by Anthony Broad to have been converted to his cause. He came into Parliament for Wycombe on the 28th July, 1646, and was allowed, for his services, from the 26th June, 1643, 9,016*l.*, which was to be paid to him out of the Excise, and from the receipts of Goldsmiths' Hall.[2]

He was a man of great influence with the Presbyterians, and, possibly in that interest, was elected Sheriff of London for the year 1647–48. He was, however, put out of his office upon the accusation of the Commons, that he had aided the invasion of the Scots in favour of the King, was arrested and expelled the House, in December, 1648, bearing for some years the penalty of his supposed treason to the Parliament (*g*, vol. 7, page 1384).

In May, 1648, broke out what was termed the Second War in favour of the King, and risings took place in Kent and Wales, the Scottish army also entering the Kingdom in July. On the whole the feeling in favour of the King gained strength in London during Warner's mayoralty. In October (*l*, page 210) originated, the proposals which were embodied in the document styled, " The agreement of the people for a compromise,"[3] and to secure a

---

[1] *k*, page 978, and 6 Rept. II. M. S. L., page 98.—*b.*

[2] His life up to this date is found in England's Worthies, by John Vicars (1647, and reprinted in 1845).—*e*, vol. 5, page 477.

[3] Printed in Appendix, *i*, page 607, as presented to the army, October 28, 1647.

lasting peace. Under this the King would have been deposed, but there arose a party, of which we may fairly presume Reynardson[1] was one of the promoters, who desired to save Charles from this degradation.

The Christmas in this year evidenced widespread discontent with the existing state of affairs. The churches in London were again adorned with rosemary and bay; the Apprentices decorated the Cornhill pump with holly and ivy, and the officers sent to remove these were driven back, chased through the streets, and Warner had to intervene in person to restore order (*l*, page 282).

As the Coronation Day (March 27th) approached, this feeling had vastly increased (*l*, page 336). More bonfires were lit in the City on this anniversary (1648) than at any time since Charles' return from Spain. All passing through the streets in carriages were compelled to drink his health, and shouts for the King were raised, and execrations poured upon his enemies.[2] A few days later, on Sunday, the 9th of April (*l*, page 340), Warner sent the train bands to prevent some boys playing "tip-cat" in Moorfields. The soldiers were disarmed, and the rioters, some 3,000 or 4,000 strong, shouted "Now for King Charles," and marched westward. This rioting continued on the 10th, and was looked upon as so serious, that the Common Council put forth, on the 11th, a statement of the circumstances, which they ordered to be read in all churches on the next Sunday, with a thanksgiving for the deliverance of the City from the rioters.[3]

On the 18th of May another Ordinance for governing the London Militia was passed, in which the Lord Mayor and Sheriffs for the time being, and Reynardson, with eight other Aldermen, were named Commissioners.[4] Peace was desired by the citizens, and this feeling again found expression in the proposal of June (*l*, page 391; *f*, page 986), to open up a "personal Treaty" with the King. On July 12th a petition for peace was sent to the Commons;[5] but this desire was not accepted by all the citizens, for on the 27th

---

[1] He was appointed by Ordinance of November one of the Commissioners for the City Assessments —(6 Reps. H. M. S.).—*a*, page 212.

[2] See Marshall's sermon of the 27th of July (*post*).

[3] Act and Declaration of the Common Council, printed London, April 14, 1648, by Husband, printer to the H. of C.; and The Rising and Rioting of the Mutineers, London, 1648, H. B., Old Bailey; also Narrative of Rioters' Tumult, London, 1648, P. Wright, King's Head, Old Bailey.

[4] Warner, Lord Mayor.—Aldermen Wollaston, Reynardson, Clarke, Gibbs, Chambers, Foot, Avery, Byde, and Viner. The Ordinance was printed by John Wright, 1648.

[5] Printed by Husband on July 14, 1648.—Heath, pages 181—184.

a "Thanksgiving Sermon" was preached at St. Paul's before Warner and the Corporation, upon the occasion of "the many late and signal victories and deliverances vouchsafed to the Parliamentary forces." The preacher was Stephen Marshall, on the text of Isaiah ix, verses 4 and 5, and from such a sermon and from such a preacher we may gather something of the spirit of the times which immediately preceded Reynardson's mayoralty.[1]

Addressing the Royalists as "Malignant Spirits": "If any such hear me this day, flatter not yourselves that you shall be able to do any great matters against the servants of Christ; your plots will all come to nothing."[2] Then, turning to the Anti-Royalists, "Who art the Lord's people," he gave them encouragement: "Lay not to heart overmuch the dangers from the hands of those who would destroy you. We are often told, '*You are not far from hanging; you must shortly look for it; England will be too hot to hold you; your doors are marked; you are known well enough; the day is coming; you will be caught ere long.*' So much rage and fury is throughout the land against them (the Lord's people), if Satan had the ruling of the roost there would not be a godly man left before to-morrow night."

Possibly an apology may be thought necessary to the reader for quoting here and elsewhere from a sermon; but the pulpit was a strong organ in influencing public opinion at a time when the newspapers can scarcely be said to have existed, for the daily and weekly press originated, according to Neal,[3] in the separation of the King and Parliament and the imposition of the negative oath of 15th April, 1642, Mercurius Auticus espousing the King's, and Mercurius Britannicus the Parliamentary, cause.

Reynardson was the first Devonshire man[4] elected to the office of Lord Mayor, and probably no Alderman entered upon this duty at a graver period of history. There were two parties in the Corporation and in Parliament: those who earnestly sought to save the King's life and throne, and others who wanted to destroy both. The Corporation had ceased, for some time past, to be independent, but was under the control, first of the Rump, and then of the army, when that dominated over England.

Of his election no entry is to be found in the Corporation

---

[1] See Lord Holles' comments on this occasion.— C. W. Tracts, vol. 1, page 286.
[2] Pages 25 and 27.
[3] History of the Parliament, vol. 2, page 475.
[4] Fuller's Worthies, page 216.

Records, but the election sermon dedicated to him as Lord Mayor
elect is extant,[1] the preacher being Obadiah Sedgwick,[2] and none
then better worth listening to. In his earlier life he served as a
Chaplain with the Parliamentary army in the west, and his minis-
terial work there must not be overlooked. A soldier-citizen writes
to his former master in London from the camp at Worcester on the
26th September, 1642, giving a diary of events, and thus describes
his Sunday :—"Sabbath day was peaceably enjoyed with Obadiah
Sedgwick, who gave two heavenly sermons ;" and again, after
giving us in greater detail a service which was held in the cathedral,
he continues that, after leaving it, "finding the shops open and men
at work, to whom we gave some plain exhortation, we went to hear
Mr. Sedgwick, who gave us two famous sermons which much affected
the poor inhabitants, who, wondering, said they had never heard the
like before, and I believe them."[3] Sedgwick was a man of large experience in the controversy of past years, for early in life he held
a church in Bread Street ; he often spoke in the City—preached
before Parliament, and held, at this date, St. Paul's, Covent Garden.
As a leader of the Presbyterian clergy, he visited the King at the
Isle of Wight, to enforce upon him his views on the Revelation of
St. John.[4] He was adverse to extreme measures against Charles,
and, on the 28th of January (Sunday), he wrote a letter to save
his life, which Cromwell described "as that of a rascally priest,"
having in the earlier part of the same sermon called Sedgwick
"the fast and loose priest of Covent Garden."[5] He was, therefore,
no friend or follower of Cromwell ; but, assuming he knew that
Reynardson would be the Lord Mayor elected, his testimony to
his "singular wisdom and expedient meekness" is emphatic.

The preacher first exhorts the citizens as *electors.* Election
he emphasised as "an action which depends upon judgment,
counsel, and deliberation. There are some magistrates by *succession*, whom people receive, but choose not, and there are some by

---

[1] Preached September 29, 1648, on Prov. 29, v. 2, printed by Peter Cole,
Cornhill, 1648.

[2].Wood's Athenæ (Bliss, 1820), vol. 3, page 441.

[3] Letters of Nehemiah Wharton to his late master, George Wittingham, Merchant, of the Golden Anchor in St. Swithin's Lane.—*d*, pages 391 and 400.

[4] Leaves of the Tree of Life, chap. 22, v. 2 ; Herbert, page 67 ; Warwick, page
308. "He held the King so late at night that, civilly thanking him for his good
will and pains, the King prayed to conclude and go to bed, for he must needs want
sleep after such a journey."

[5] Sermon by Cromwell, April, 1649, at Sir Peter Temple's, in Lincoln's Inn
Fields, vol. 4 ; *e*, History of Independents, page 153 ; Harleian Miscellany, pages
178—179.

nomination, who are chosen for us, but not by us, and there are some magistrates by *election,* who are (if I may so allude) our own creatures or workmanship. . . O, therefore, how serious should you be in this work. . . . Since the office is high, the trust great, the administration difficult, the error dangerous, the opportunity honourable, and the action weighty ; here are reasons why you should be serious."

" Beloved, you have in your hands this one day all the next year's mercies or blessings—all your own comforts and all your brethren's comforts. A good choice is a full year's blessing. And verily, as such an opportunity is precious, so the honour which God puts upon you in that opportunity is very glorious; for as the magistrates are God's in respect of office, so are you (who come to choose) also God's in respect to the fruit of your choice, for, according as your choice is, you make day or night, light or darkness, good or evil, joy or sorrow, unto the people : which works God owns for his works, in Scripture."

He then counselled them to choose the new magistrate, (1) by book, *i.e.,* the Bible, (2) on your knees, and (3) by your votes.

Next adverting to the present temper of the times and addressing the Lord Mayor to be elected, he continues thus :—

" SIR—

" As your choice, so your work is likely to be, in a troublesome time. You well know how divided, how broken, how shivered, our public condition is; and when the ship is in broken seas the danger is the greater, and the pilot hath more reason to be careful and circumspect. . . . Sir, though it is some part of your unhappiness to appear upon the stage in divided and distempered times, yet it will be more for your honour if you can, with your singular wisdom and expedient meekness, calm our seas, quench our fires, bind us all up into an amity and love who are started asunder so much through our own frailties, and (I fancy) the more through other men's subtleties. One reports of Hippocrates that he gave an oath unto his scholars to look well to his children . . . and I would commend into your choisest care two children, and both of them belong to God . . . to nurse them for one year: the one is Religion, the other is Justice. If you look well to them you may be confident that God will look well to you. These are the two legs upon which the political body stands—nay, they are the two pillars which hold up heaven and earth."

The first entry relating to Reynardson's mayoralty is to be

found in the Merchant Taylors' Records. On the 18th of October his election is referred to by a vote of 100 marks to "trim his Lordship's house," and the use of the Company's plate during his year of office.[1] None of the other courtesies offered to a Lord Mayor by his Company are noticed; as the good old custom of hospitality on St. Simon and St. Jude's Day, and the grand procession[2] of joyous citizens to Westminster no longer were observed. The second entry is on the Corporation Records of the 7th of November, when he is entered as presiding as Lord Mayor.

We must now trace as briefly as possible, first, the political events happening in the year of his mayoralty, which led to the subversion of all authority save that of the army, and then the changes made in the House of Commons and in the Corporation of London, whereby Charles I was brought to the scaffold.

While negotiations for peace and a settlement of the Kingdom were pending, the army again advanced upon London and demanded of Parliament "that the person of the King may be proceeded against in a due way of justice," and of the Lord Mayor and citizens that the army should be provided for (g, page 1341).

Fairfax wrote on the 30th of November, stating his intention to dispose of his men, not in private, but in great and void, houses about the City, at the same time telling the citizens that they might avoid even this inconvenience by paying up, "before to-morrow night if possible," 40,000l. which was due to the army (g, page 1349).

This letter reached Reynardson on the same night, and, though addressed "to the Lord Mayor, Aldermen, and Common Council," was opened by him in the presence of the Sheriffs. The Common Council had it submitted to them on the 1st of December, "when it was questioned by some of the members of the Court whether

---

[1] " Whereas Alderman Reynardson, a worthy member and brother of this Company, is lately elected to the office of Lord Mayor of this City for the year ensuing, this Court doth think fit to present his Lordship with some gratuity as a token of the Company's love towards the trimming up of his Lordship's house, and thereupon, with general consent, it is ordered that there shall be bestowed upon his Lordship the sum of 100 marks, being the like sum which was formerly given to Sir John Gore and also to Sir Robert Ducie in the several times of their mayoralties, and for the payment thereof this order to be our Master's discharge, and this Court doth further order that his Lordship, if he please, be accommodated with such of the Company's plate as they can spare, and as his Lordship will have occasion to use during his mayoralty."

[2] b, page 242. The show (and probably the dinner) ceased from 1639 to 1655. See Nichol's London Pageants, page 103.

his Lordship ought to open the same or not, being directed as aforesaid, and, being put to the question, it was voted that his Lordship did well in what he did in opening the said letter " (*a*). From thence it was sent to the Commons, who, after a long debate, closing at 8 P.M., declared that the City should provide the 40,000*l*.

On the 5th, the Commons voted, by 129 to 83, that the King's answers to their proposals were a ground for proceeding with the treaty with him, but the army entered the suburbs, and as they had no accommodation, sleeping on boards, with but little firing, beds were not unreasonably demanded from the City, if the soldiers were to be kept out of private houses (*g*, page 1353).

Having gained military occupation of London, the army began at once to expel all the King's supporters from the House of Commons. With this object, Colonel Pride stood at the door on the 6th, and, as the members proposed to enter, stopped some and imprisoned others,[1] so that the House was but a rump of its former members. On the 8th, Fairfax swept the treasuries in Goldsmiths', Haberdashers', and Weavers' Halls of their contents, finding in the latter 2,000*l*.[2] He also quartered his soldiers in Blackfriars, Ludgate, and St. Paul's (*g*, page 1356), and, on the 9th, brought a regiment of horse and quartered them in private houses (*g*, page 1358).[3]

While the army was thus pressing for the speedy execution of justice against the King, a new representation, said to have been drafted by Ireton for the establishment of a firm and lasting peace, to be subscribed throughout the Kingdom, which did not ask for the King's deposition, was presented to the Commons, who, according to Evelyn, sat up the whole night of the 13th to conclude the treaty, but were dispersed by the army.[4] A meeting was held at the Rolls House after the Chancery business of the day (18th of December) was over, at which Richard Deane and Cromwell attended to meet the Speaker, the Keeper of the Great Seal (Widdrington), and Whitelock. Such persons, no doubt, met, and

---

[1] Rushworth gives the names of 41 who were seized (*g*, page 1355), but the army interdicted 143 members from voting. The decision on the 7th to proceed with the proposal of the army was 28 against 50.—C. J., 6, page 95.

[2] His letter, printed on December 9, 1648, by Field, London.

[3] By Fairfax's order of December 28, Merchant Taylors' Hall was protected from the billetting of horse and foot soldiers, obtained by the Quartermaster-General being a member of the Company and receiving 20*l*. and for his man 10*s*.—*i*, pages 579—580; *l*, page 551; *h*, page 361; and *g*, vol. 7, page 1392.

[4] Evelyn's Diary, vol. 1, page 227.

adjourned for another meeting (*h*), but it is stated by an authority which may be deemed sufficient that the Lord Mayor was also present, and that the subject discussed was the settlement of the Kingdom upon the basis of deposing the King and raising the young Duke of Gloucester to the throne.[1]

To advert to the changes about to be made relating to the Corporation. The citizens who had elected Reynardson as Lord Mayor were, as Guildsmen, and also as citizens, sworn liegemen of the King, and their oaths were cumulative—that is, at each stage of their corporate life, from being Freemen to becoming (if such) Lord Mayor they had sworn allegiance to their Sovereign by oaths,[2] then as now, the same as are to be found in the Statute Book of Edward III.

The Common Council then, as now, held office for one year, being elected on St. Thomas' Day at Wardmotes presided over by the Alderman of each ward (*j*, vol. I, pages 11—32). The first measure passed was to disfranchise all the Royalists from voting for, and to disqualify them from holding, office. Thus, by Ordinance of the 20th December, all those who had subscribed any engagement in the year 1648, relating to "the personal Treaty with the King," were not either to vote for, or to be elected to, any office in the City (*c*, pages 98—101).

This dislocated all the existing City organisations, and, upon the 23rd, the Lord Mayor and Aldermen presented a petition by Alderman Viner to the Commons (*c*, page 103), setting forth that the citizens were so generally engaged in the petition for a personal Treaty, that all the old Common Councilmen whom they were to elect on the 21st were generally so engaged therein, that they could not, with such restriction, find men enough to elect, or who would stand for election (*g*, page 1370); but the House refused to interfere, and ordered an election to be forthwith made under their law, also that the "illegal oaths," as they were pleased to call them, "of allegiance and supremacy," and all others of a like nature, taken by Freemen, should be referred to a committee of their own House for abolition (*g*, pages 109 and 1376).

Thus, with this emphatic warning of the temper of the men with whom he would have to contend, Reynardson entered upon

---

[1] The Life of Richard Deane, by J. B. Deane, F.S.A., London, 1870, pages 337—339.

[2] Compare those printed in Statutes of the Realm, vol. 1, page 349, and in the Report on Oaths, 1867.

his single-handed contest with the Rump[1] and their supporters in the City. The oaths had not been altered, and therefore he refused (*g*, page 1334) to let any man take his seat in the Common Council without swearing the oath of allegiance. Complaint was immediately made against him to the House, and, on the 5th of January, he was ordered to summon the Common Council together, and to require them to do their duty, but to suspend the taking of oaths (*e*, pages 111—112).

As it was possible that such an order might lead to some breach of the peace, the House further ordered Reynardson to take down within the City and the suburbs all the chains which had been placed there originally as a protection to the citizens from cavalry charges. Ven (*e*, page 113) was to communicate these orders to the Lord Mayor and to bring in two Ordinances : one for the resettling of the City Militia, and the other for removing obstructions in the election of City officers.

On the 23rd December the Commons had appointed a Committee " to consider how to proceed, by way of justice, against the King and other capital offenders," which, on the 2nd of January, led to a difference with the Lords (12 Peers constituting the House) ; thereupon the Commons assumed (*e*, pages 109—110 ; *h*, page 367) to themselves the power of acting without the Lords' concurrence, and, on the 4th, " declared that they were the supreme power in the nation," and, as such, passed, on the 8th, what they called " an Act "[2] for erecting a Court of Justice, which led to the King's execution.

This Act was proclaimed at the Exchange and in Cheapside not by Reynardson, but by the Serjeant-at-Arms with the Commons' mace upon his shoulder, and all persons were invited to bring in their charges (*g*, page 1387 ; *h*, page 367) against the King. Then, to secure the safety of the dominant party, and to prevent any popular movement in London on behalf of the King, a general order of the 9th of January was issued by Fairfax, from his headquarters in Queen Street, for all persons who had engaged in the first or second war, and had adhered unto or assisted the King or his party therein, to depart from London or within 10 miles thereof

---

[1] I use the term for the " Little Parliament," as Carlyle defines it.—Cromwell's Letters, vol. 2, page 351.

[2] *e*, pages 111—113. About this time, Whitelock states, the Rump used " Act " in lieu of " Ordinance."—*h*, page 369.

in 24 hours, and not to return thereto for the space of one month, at the peril of being arrested and dealt with as prisoners of war (*g*, page 1388).

The Rump having thus purged the City, as well as Parliament, of all Royalists, the proposals to bring the King to trial, which had been initiated at Westminster, were to find approval in the City; for if London, acting with the supreme authority of the Corporation, would endorse this policy of the Rump, such a fact would immensely strengthen them in their course of action, and go far to persuade the world that the trial of the King by his accusers had received the deliberate approval of the people of England.

Accordingly a petition was put in circulation, to be signed by any who pleased, addressed to the Commons, in these words :—

" 1. That, as ye have begun to advance the interest of impartial justice, so you would vigorously proceed in the execution thereof upon all the grand and capital authors, contrivers of, and actors in, the late wars against the Parliament and Kingdom, from the highest to the lowest. That the wrath of God may be appeased, good men satisfied, and evil men deterred from adventuring upon the like practices for the future."

And concluding thus :—

" 5. That, having by your votes of the 4th of January instant, '*declared that the Commons of England, in Parliament assembled, have the supreme power of this nation,*' you would (as far as you are able) endeavour the settling thereof upon foundations of righteousness and peace. In the maintenance and prosecution of which votes, and of these our just and humble desires, we are resolved to stand by you to the uttermost of our power against all opposition whatsoever."

In order to give weight and authority to this petition, the promoters designed to obtain its adoption by the newly-formed Common Council which Reynardson had been ordered to summon. Accordingly, on the 9th, when the Council met, Reynardson having the support of six only of the Aldermen,[1] the petition was submitted, with the request that it might be presented by them to the House of Commons. After it had been openly read, the Court, perceiving its importance, referred it to a special Committee " to

---

[1] These were Edmunds, Avery (Merchant Taylor), Bide, Viner, Packe, and Bateman.

take the same into their sad and serious consideration, and to report to the Court, in writing, their opinions thereon."[1]

The contents of the petition thus became known to Reynardson, and he had to determine alone, or at least with few only of his brethren, what course he should take for the honour of the City. The intention of the petitioners, and of those who aided them, was clearly not merely to dethrone, but to destroy the King. To put such a petition to the vote in this newly-formed Common Council was to invite disaster. All, therefore, that could be done was for him to preside, as Lord Mayor, and refuse to allow the question of receiving the petition to be put; and this he determined to do.

The Corporation Records contain no entry made, on the 13th of January, of the Council held upon that day. The time of meeting was 8 A.M., but it was, and still is, usual for the Aldermen to assemble first in their own room, and to go thence with the Lord Mayor, preceded by the sword and mace bearers and other officers. In this instance the Lord Mayor did not enter till 11 o'clock A.M., and only two of the Aldermen accompanied him. The meeting commences when the Lord Mayor is seated and the sword and mace[2] are placed on the table before him, and closes when these are withdrawn and he leaves the Council.[3] The Lord Mayor has the general control of the meeting.

Of what passed on this occasion we have two accounts: the first by Smallwood, which runs thus :—

---

[1] The entry in the Corporation Records is in these words :—

"At this Common Council divers Freemen of the City of London did prefer their petition by them subscribed, directed to the Honourable the Lord Mayor, Aldermen, and Common Council of the City of London, in Common Council assembled, whereby they desire that their petition thereunto annexed, subscribed by many hands, directed to the Honourable the Commons of England in Parliament assembled, might be presented by this Court to the said Honourable House of Commons. The which said petitions were here openly read, and this Court upon the reading thereof did conceive the same to be matter of high concernment. And therefore it is ordered that Sir John Wollaston, Knight and Alderman, Mr. Alderman Andrews, Mr. Alderman Gibbs, and Mr. Alderman Packe, or any two of them, Mr. Russell, Coll. Titchbourn, Mr. Moyer, Mr. Hilslen, Mr. Shute, Mr. Pennoyer, Mr. Eastwicke, and Mr. Daniell Taylor, or any four of them shall forthwith meet together, and take the said petition into their sad and serious consideration. And thereupon to report to this Court in writing their opinions concerning the same and what they shall think fit to be done thereupon, that this Court upon their said report may give such further directions therein as they shall think fit. And Thomas Blinkensof to warn and attend them."

[2] The insignia of office are the sceptre, sword, and mace.

[3] Hatsell (vol. 2, page 141, note) thus states the Rule of Parliament :—When the mace lies on the table, it is a House ; when under the table a committee ; when out of the House no business can be done ; when from the table and on the Ser-

E

" When some tumultuous and base Commoners[1] had conceived a traitorous and wicked petition to bring his sacred Majesty and others to tryal, and were vehemently urgent to have it read and voted in the Common Council that it might be presented to the new-moulded Parliament as the desire of the whole City, this heroic and noble knight opposed the promoting thereof, and would suffer it not either to be read or voted, notwithstanding the rage and violence of the adverse party . . . loading him with reproach and contempt within, telling him that they would have it voted before their rising, and some of them stirred up a tumultuous rabble against him without. Notwithstanding, he continued like an immovable rock, persisting in his resolution, and endured their insolences " from 8 A.M. till after 8 P.M., " accompanied only by two of his brethren, and would not yield a jot to their unreasonable desires, notwithstanding all their clamorous importunities ; and, at last, when no reason would prevail with them, nor longer able to endure their uncivil behaviour, but chiefly that he might, to the utmost of his power, keep the City and citizens from being stained with the guilt of that sacred eminent blood, he resolutely took up the sword and departed the Court to his great hazard." [2]

The other is the account which was prepared by the Commons of London and presented to the Rump (*a*).

" About 11 of the clock the Lord Mayor, accompanied only with two of the Aldermen, took the chayre. We then desiring the Lord Mayor that the acts of the last Court might be read according to the usual course of the said Court, and for the further confirmation of the said acts, could not obtain the same (though earnestly desired) for above an hour's space. After which some members of the said Court (being part of a Committee formerly chosen by the said Court) tendered a petition thereunto to be read and considered of, which petition (being the same now presented to this Honourable House) was drawn up by them in reference to an order of the said Court, and received the approbation of the major part of the quorum of that Committee, and though it was often and earnestly pressed for a long time by the major part of the Court, that it might be read to receive the sense of the

---

jeant's shoulder at the Bar, the Speaker only can manage, and no motion can be made.—See Fenwick's Case, 13 State Trials, pages 544—546.

[1] Maitland (vol. 1, page 419) refers to this incident, but with so little appreciation of the facts, that he names *Warner* as the Lord Mayor occupying the chair. See also 2 Entick, page 233.

[2] Appendix II.

Court, yet the Lord Mayor wholly refused to suffer the same or that the question should be put whether it should be read, aye or noe. After the fruitless expense of many hours, another question being drawn up, the major part of the Court required it to be put, to be decided according to the right and custom of the Court, and being denied therein, declared how unjust and of what destructive nature to the being of the Court such a deniall would be, yet, notwithstanding, the Lord Mayor, with the two Aldermen, departed and left the Court sitting, to the great griefe and general dissatisfaction of the same. Being thus deprived of our ordinary assistance for our proceedings we did then require and command the Common Serjeant and Town Clerk, officers of the said Court, to stay in the Court and put the question, both which they contemptuously refused, and left the Court sitting likewise."

Thus, after many hours of conflict with the Commons of London, carried on with inflexible resolution, Reynardson closed the meeting, having saved the Corporation from the supreme act of disloyalty in which his opponents sought to involve their fellow-citizens.

The narrative went on to describe Reynardson's conduct as inflicting "sufferings for eight hours at least, in breach of undoubted rights and privileges," and appealed to the House "for the consideration thereof, and for such directions as might make the Commons of London useful for the ends for which they were chosen."

So far as I know there is no record extant giving the names of the two Aldermen who adhered to Reynardson on this occasion. On the Court there were five[1] appointed in the Ordinance for, and acted as judges at, the King's trial, and six[2] others were ultimately degraded for their adherence to his cause. Two of these, Soames and Chambers, were summoned before the Rump,[3] and declared, as Reynardson had done, that their oaths of allegiance restrained them from acting against the King's authority. Another Alderman, "Honest Avery,"[4] was his colleague on the Court of the Mer-

---

[1] Pennington, Atkins, Wilson, Fowke, Andrews.—*j*, page 1383.
[2] Gayre, Adams, Langham, Soames, Bunce, Chambers.—*e*, page 117.
[3] Lloyd's Memoir, 1668, page 630, and *e*, page 222.
[4] Lloyd's Memoir, page 630.—*d*, 1659, pages 569—611.

Samuel, son of James Avery, of Mells, in the county of Somerset, Clothier, was apprenticed to Richard Gore, Merchant Taylor of London and Merchant Adventurer to Spain and Portugal, on February 5, 1609, and made free by servitude on February 11, 1621. Being elected an Alderman, he was sworn as an Assistant, and

chaut Taylors, but took office under the Council of State, and is not likely to have been one of the two adhering to Reynardson.

To complete the history of this eventful day, it may be stated that after Reynardson had left the chair, Colonel Owen Rowe was voted into it, who took a prominent part in City affairs and was the deputy of the Alderman of Coleman Street Ward. From being Sergeant-Major he had become Colonel of the 5th City Regiment.[1] According to his own account of himself " he was not brought up a scholar but a tradesman," and pleaded ignorance for the acts charged against him, when tried as a regicide.[2] However, the petition from the Commons of London (the names of the Lord Mayor and Aldermen having been omitted) to the Commons of England was carried with these resolutions:— That a deputation .of 20 members should present the same "in their gowns"—Colonels Rowe and Titchborne being members thereof. That a narrative (which we have already quoted) should be forthwith prepared, voted, and presented with the petition. That four coaches should be ready on Monday at the Guildhall to carry the 20 persons to Westminster. They or any five to be a committee to attend the pleasure of the House touching the said narrative (*a*).

Accordingly on Monday they went to Westminster, as we find from the Commons' Journal :—

"Jan. 15th.—The House (*e*, pages 112—118; *g*, pages 1301; *h*, page 369) being informed that divers of the Common Council of the City of London were at the door; they were called in, and Colonel Titchborne,[3] in the name of the City of London, made a short preamble to this effect : 'Mr. Speaker, the Commons of the City of London in Common Council assembled desired these gentlemen and myself to wait on you this morning to present to this Honourable House their humble petition, in which I should not spend your time but that the title varies from others of the like nature which have been formerly presented. The title wants the names of the " Lord Mayor and Aldermen." For the reasons of that omission the Commons have spoken their own sense in a " narrative " which they annex to this petition.

---

also elected and sworn as Master of the Company on July 15, 1645. He was Sheriff in 1647.

[1] 50 Archd., page 24.

[2] *k*, vol. 5, page 1204. See the speech on his trial, *k*, V., page 1203.

[3] Lord Mayor in 1656, and tried as a regicide.

Howsoever, the Commons would not omit the presenting of the petition, lest we should be thought to be men forgetting the duty we owe and to have lost our first love. I shall only say we are the same men we were, and what we have engaged for with you, we shall still engage with the same constancy. Within these 7 years past we have had a greater light and discovery of men and things. Our petition speaks our desires; the narrative of our grievances; and ourselves yours to live and die with you.'

"The petition and narrative being read, it was resolved that the Commons of England in Parliament do declare that the petition and narrative presented by order may and of right ought to be entered in the books and among the acts of the Common Council there." The petitioners were then called in and thanked by the Speaker, who added: "I am withal to tell you that the House doth approve of your acting and resolving by yourselves at a Common Council, in case of absence or dissent in the Lord Mayor or Aldermen or both together." The papers were to be printed,[1] but no order, probably to the chagrin of the deputation, was made against Reynardson.

After this episode the Rump resumed their measures for the reform of the Corporation. They ordered Reynardson to send up the Book of Oaths (c) for revision, and having given authority to the Common Council to perform their duty unsworn, they resolved on the 13th that the words, "Ye shall be true to our Sovereign Lord the King that now is, and to his heirs and successors, Kings of England" should be omitted from the oath taken by City officers,[2] and shortly after the Freeman's Oaths of Allegiance and Supremacy were abolished (e, page 116).

But, though great, these changes were not all that were made. Having swept away the King and Lords from Parliament, it would have been consistent to have abolished the Lord Mayor and Aldermen from the Corporation, but this they did not venture upon.

A Common Council could not be legally held without a summons[3] from the Lord Mayor, and his presiding (either himself or by his deputy), with the sword, mace, or other insignia of authority, lying on the table before him; for when, in 1642, the

---

[1] By Cole, Royal Exchange, January 16, 1648.
[2] Scobel's Ordinances for 1648, caps. 7 and 8.—e.
[3] Bohun's Priviledgia, London (1722), page 377.

Commons wanted a deputy appointed, the Aldermen on July 20th certified to the House that the Lord Mayor *only* had the authority to make such an appointment (*k*, page 164).

As to the sword and other insignia of office (*j*, page 336), the possession of these as an evidence of authority was of the highest importance.[1]   For the King to take the sword from the Lord Mayor was to depose him (*j*, vol. 2, page 110).   So when Gurney was illegally deposed he refused to give up the insignia to any save the King (*k*, page 164).   Gayre, when he was imprisoned, on the 25th of September, 1647, took them with him to the Tower (*k*, page 600), and, doubtless, Reynardson would have done the same had not the Council "forthwith sent for them."   After the abolition of the kingly office, the civic sword, when the Speaker came into the City, was given to him, as in June, 1649, when the Rump dined at Grocers' Hall.   He received and redelivered the sword to the Lord Mayor, who bore it himself before the Speaker until they entered the Hall.[2]   When Cromwell dissolved the Long Parliament on the 20th April, 1653, he did so by putting into safe custody not the Speaker, but the mace.   An Ordinance was therefore passed authorising any six Common Councilmen to send a requisition to the Lord Mayor to call a Council, and, should he fail to do so, to call such themselves, and thereat any 40 members should have the power to act without the Lord Mayor's presence.[3]

The King was beheaded on the 30th January, and the Rump on the 31st (*c*) referred it to "a Committee to bring in an Act for the tryal of delinquents."   Reynardson, knowing how elastic that term was, and how many of his friends might be tried as such for the efforts they had made to save the King's life by the "Personal Treaty," at once destroyed it.   "In reference to the good of the City, whereof he was Chief Magistrate," said Smallwood, at Reynardson's funeral, "when a Treaty was concluded upon between his late Majesty of Blessed Memory and the Parliament then sitting, and in order thereunto an engagement was subscribed by most of the Common Council and principal members of the City for the carrying on of that Treaty.   Afterwards the Treaty proving ineffectual, and the Parliament being dissolved by

---

[1] Cromwell's Letters, by Carlyle, vol. 2, page 382.
[2] *d*, 1649-50, page 174—5.
[3] No such Ordinance is to be found in Scobel, but is entered on the Corporation Records.—*e* and *g*.

the unjust violence of the army and their abettors, a strict inquiry was made after the names of those that subscribed the Personal Treaty. But the book wherein the names of the subscribers on both parts for and against the Treaty were written, containing about two reams of paper, being privately brought to this worthy knight, then Lord Mayor, he, tendering the good and welfare of all his brethren and fellow citizens, not knowing what might be the ill consequences of it, if such a record should be found extant, took it and burnt it to ashes privately in his chamber, that nothing might remain to the prejudice of any." Then, appealing to the mourners, he continued, "How many perhaps here present were deeply engaged to him for the safety of their estates, if not of their lives by that one action? Certainly it was a work full of wisdom, charity, and brotherly kindness, a most excellent concatenation of Christian graces."[1]

About this period of which we are writing the office of "President to St. Bartholomew's Hospital" became vacant, and was by right or courtesy offered to, and accepted by, Reynardson,[2] thus:—

> "23rd die February, Anno Dom. 1648.
> "Raynardson, President.

"This day the right Honorable Abraham Raynardson, the Lord Mayor of the Citty of London was by elecion and scrutany of this Co[rt] chosen to be President of this Hospital in the roome and place of S[r] George Clarke, late K[nt], deceased: wheruppon it was desired that Mr. Harrison Chamblane, Mr. Johnson, Mr. Deputy Morrell, Mr. Luster, Mr. Norton, and Mr. Ashwell should attend his Lordshipp, to knowe his pleasure herein; who did at the same Co[rt] declare his answere, that his Lordshipp did accept thereof and gave them thankes and that he would doe this house the best service he could."

On the day preceding, a Court of Common Council had been held to appoint Stephen Marshall to preach the Spittle Sermon on Easter Monday, but no reference to the incidents of the 13th of January is found until the Court of the 17th of March, when this order was made: "That an Act of the Commons of England

---

[1] Appendix III.
[2] Memoranda relating to the Royal Hospitals (London, 1863).—c. I am indebted to Mr. Cross, of the Hospital, for these minutes.

made the 28th of February last, and now read in this Court, concerning the proceedings at the last Common Council holden the 13th day of January last past and for the proceedings of this Court for the future shall be entered in the Book of Common Council. The tenor of which said Act of the Commons of England, together with the proceedings of the Common Council holden the said 13th day of January last, followeth in these words."[1] Then were placed on record the petition and narrative already quoted (*a*).

On the same day on which this Court was held, an Act was passed for abolishing the kingly office,[2] which was sent on the 23rd by Alderman Pennington to Reynardson for him to proclaim in the City. It was left at his house in Bishopsgate Street with his wife, and the reception she gave the messenger was one of defiance.[3] "This lady not suffering him that brought the order to drink in her house (evidencing the then prevailing custom of the City), but bidding him to return to his masters for his wages."

The duty thus sought to be imposed was not one pertaining to the office of Lord Mayor or one which Reynardson could honestly discharge. No one knew better, or more fully appreciated the fact, that he had been elected by Royalists (of which the representation of the 23rd of December will assure the reader), and that upon entering into office, he had, besides the mere oath of allegiance, specially sworn "as Lord Mayor" to give "true and lawful service," and "surely and safely to keep the City for the King of England" (*j*, page 23). It was a triumphant insult to the Royalists of the City, and, happen what may, he had resolved to obey his conscience, and not carry out the behests of Pennington and the Rump.

But the account of him, as Lord Mayor, which I am about to

---

[1] The members present were :

A. Reynardson, Mayor.

Sir J. Wollaston.	Thomas Andrews.	
John Fowke.	Thomas Foote.	
John Kendrick.	Thomas Cullum.	Aldermen.
Symon Edmunds.	John Byde.	
Richard Bateman.	John Benticke.	

[2] *g*, page 389 ; Scobel, cap. 16 ; *e*, page 177.

[3] Heath's Chronicle of the Civil Wars (1676), page 231 ; Lloyd's Memoirs, page 630.

close, would not be complete without mentioning, as emphasising the character of the man, the gift which he made to the parish of St. Martin.[1] With its church,[2] the advowson of which was given to the Taylors, in 1404, he was linked by a twofold interest. There as guildsman he had for years past celebrated the annual festival of his Company on St. John the Baptist's Day, before electing the Master and Wardens; and there the almsmen living adjacent were to be "personally present in the said church, there serving God and keeping all Divine service said and sung, and praying every day for the fraternity and the benefactors thereof.[3] As a parishioner, the church was a place not only of his worship but of his sepulture, for several of his children[4] and himself afterwards were buried therein.

This gift was of Communion vessels which are thus entered in the church registers:[5] "Two silver flaggons and two gilt cups with covers. Both the flaggons hath engraven thereon, 'This and one other flaggon was given by Abraham Reynardson, Lord Mayor of London, to the parish church of St. Martin Outwich for the Communion Table. 1648.' And each of the said flaggons hath the arms of the said Abraham Reynardson engraven thereon described. One of which weighing 55 ozs. 7 dwts., and the other 54 ozs. 15 dwts."[6]

To revert to the concluding acts of his mayoralty. On the 29th he held what proved to be the last civic court over which he was ever to preside; for he did not proclaim the abolition of the kingly office, and, on the 2nd of April, he appeared at the Bar of the House to answer for his conduct. He there admitted the receipt of the order from Alderman Pennington, and the answer

---

[1] Wilkinson's Antique Remains (London, 1797).

[2] It escaped the fire of 1666, but was pulled down in 1796, and the re-erected church was removed altogether under an Order of Council of May 5th, 1873.—*i*, pages 46 and 337.

[3] See the Ordinance set out.—*i*, page 48.

[4] In 1641-43-44-47 and 1652.—MS. addition to Wilkinson by Ellis in the Merchant Taylors' Library.

[5] I am indebted to the Rev. J. A. L. Airey, the rector, for calling my attention to this fact.

[6] From the MS. last quoted, it appears that the flagons were stolen in 1809 and never recovered. The original cost was 5*s*. 3*d*. per ounce or thereabouts, as the Saddlers' Company sold their gilt bowls and covers in 1642 at this rate.—Sherwell's History, page 91. The Guildhall Court in 1643 took in plate at 5*s*. an ounce, the ordinary price being 4*s*. 4*d*.—Cripps' Old English Plate, page 46.

he gave was "that his conscience being charged with several oaths he could not dispense with it in proclaiming the Act, and that he had not done so.[1] A long debate ensued, and, as the result of it, the House voted that for his contempt he should be (1) fined in 2,000*l.*, to be paid to the poor; (2) committed to the Tower of London for two months' imprisonment; (3) be degraded from his office of Lord Mayor.

The latter punishments could be and were carried out at once. Reynardson was sent to the Tower,[2] and the obsequious Aldermen cashiered him the same day by seizing the insignia of office. This is the entry of their proceedings : "Special Court of Aldermen, held April 2nd, 1649. Present—Wollaston, Atkin, Andrews, Fowkes, Foote, Kendrick, Culham, Edmonds, Park, Dethicks. Item : in obedience to an order of the Commons assembled in Parliament, made the 2nd day of this instant month, it is ordered by this Court that the Livery of the several Companies of this city shall be summoned according to ancient custom to meet in the Guildhall "tomorrow in the afternoon, by 2 of the clock, for the election of a new Lord Mayor, in the place of Abraham Reynardson, late Lord Mayor, and that the sword and all ensigns and ornaments of state belonging to the Lord Mayor of this city be forthwith sent for to the use and purpose in the said order mentioned."[3]

So terminated Reynardson's mayoralty, and Smallwood thus comments upon it, "He was a man of very peaceable and quiet spirit, but his fidelity and love of peace were very costly to him, for the being Lord Mayor was prejudicial to his estate at least to the value of 20,000*l.*, besides his fine, as he hath affirmed with his own hand."[4]

One of the consequences of his imprisonment was his non-attendance as President of St. Bartholomew's Hospital, and having to appoint a deputy to act for him. Thus : "Whereas Mr. Treasurer propounded the necessity for a general Co[rt] It was here upon thought fit and ordered that o[r] Clarke, W[m] Cawthorne shall

---

[1] *e*, page 177 ; *g*, page 393 ; Trial and Examination of the Lord Mayor, April 2, 1649, printed by R. Williamson. It was proclaimed by Andrews on May 30, 1650. —2 Entick, page 236.

[2] Bayley's Tower, page 580, London, 1830.

[3] He was succeeded by Thomas Andrews, a renegade, by trade a linen draper.— Heath, page 199.

[4] Appendix II, Sermon, page 34.

attend the late L. M., Alderman Raynardson, the now President, to knowe his pleasure concerning the said Co^{rt} and whither he will recomend the business of the Co^{rt} to any Alderman Gov'no^r of this Hospi^{le}, he being himselfe in restrainte as a prisoner in the Tower" (*c*, April 9th, 1649).

But whether the fine of 2,000*l.* should be paid by Reynardson rested with him, and he well decided not to yield to the Rump any acknowledgment of their authority to make such an order against him. The matter was one of higher than mere personal interest, and men rose up to protest in print against the injustice of his sentence. "A Vindication of the late Lord Mayor" was put forth, and of sufficient weight and importance to rouse the Council of State to issue an order on the 26th of April for the arrest of the author and publisher of it.[1]

Reynardson was not a poor man,[2] or one unable, if willing, to pay the fine, but his conduct was influenced by a higher motive,

---

[1] *d*, vol. 42, page 530. I have failed to find this tract in the British Museum or Bodleian Libraries, and Reynardson's family knew nothing of it.

[2] LOANS MADE BY ALDERMAN REYNARDSON TO THE MERCHANT TAYLORS' COMPANY.

Year.	Loans made by him.	Rate of interest.	Loans repaid to him.	Amount due to him.
	£		£	£
1641–42	500[1]	8 per cent.	..	500
1642–43	2,400[2]	8 "	..	..
	500[3]	7 "	..	3,400
1643–44	100	8 "	500	3,000
1644–45	..	..	600	2,400
1646–47	..	..	900	1,500
1648–49	1,000[4]	6 per cent.	..	2,500
1649–50	1,500[5]	7 "	1,000	3,000
1651–52	500[6]	5½ "	..	3,500
1652–53	500	5 "	..	..
	1,000	6 "	..	5,000
1656–57	..	..	2,500	2,500
1657–58	500	6 per cent.	..	3,000
1658–59	..	..	1,000	2,000
1659–60	500	6 per cent.	1,000	1,500

Nos. 1 and 2 were towards the 10,000*l.* assessed on the Company for the relief of Ireland.

No. 3 was for general purposes and was repaid in 1643–44.

  " 4. This bond for 1,000*l.* was, on December 5, 1649, transferred into the name of his son, A. Reynardson, Jun.

  " 5. The bond for 500*l.*, part of this loan, was, on June 9, 1650, renewed in the name of his son, A. Reynardson, Jun.

  " 6. The bond for this 500*l.* was in the name of Samuel Reynardson.

"His goods, household stuff, and wearing apparel were ordered to be sold by the candle,[1] which was done accordingly. Thus the unspotted integrity and Christian fortitude of this then Honorable Lord Mayor did shew forth most gloriously."[2]

Rumour must have reached "the Committee for advance of money,"[3] that Reynardson held some interest in the ventures of the East India Company, for an order of the 18th December, 1650, was made against them to certify to the Committee, at Haberdashers' Hall, "what money, goods, or other estate" they had belonging to him, and on the 8th of January they certified that on the 8th of November, they had received a notice of a deed of gift from him of all his right and interest in the Company to his sons, that he had an adventure of 1,200*l.* in the 4th Joint Stock, but that there had been no division of profits in respect thereof.[4]

He was, therefore, ordered to appear before the Committee, and on the 7th February, the matter was referred to another Committee "to levy the fine, and should he delay to pay, then his goods were to be seized and sold, and his rents sequestered." Accordingly one of his tenants (Rule) was ordered to pay his rent, and the East India Company to pay 1,200*l.* of their (4th) Stock to the Committee.

So matters remained until the 7th of May, 1651, when a final order was made that all Reynardson's estate was to be seized and paid to the Committee till the 2,000*l.* was paid. This, however, would seem not to have procured payment, for, on the 19th of January, 1654, he was again threatened with sequestration unless a balance of 33*l.* 5*s.* should be paid forthwith, which is

---

[1] That is, the bid at the sale became absolute when the candle expired. It was therefore an act of fraud secretly to extinguish it. See Cal. (S. P.), Advance of Monies, page viii. of Vol. 1.

[2] Appendix II.

[3] Committee for Advance of Money.—The Calendar (Domestic Series) of State Papers (1640-65), Part 3, page 1189.

[4] MS. Records of the East India Company, vol. 21, page 34. These further entries are in vol. 23 :—

> November 16, 1655. To have an account of Mr. Thos. Reynardson's delivered to him.—(*a*), vol. 23, page 239.
> August 15, 1656. Came before Court for payment of his kinsman's (Thos. Reynardson) salary, who was a factor in India.—(*b*), vol. 23, page 265.
> October 26, 1658. For bond (of Thomas Reynardson) to be cancelled.—(*e*), vol. 23, page 325.

the last entry as to the fine imposed upon him for his disobedience as Lord Mayor.

During his mayoralty he was necessarily absent from the Merchant Taylors' Court, but on the 5th of December, 1649, is entered as " Abraham Reynardson, Esq.," and placed in rank after the Aldermen, but both on the records of St. Bartholomew's and of the East India Company, he continued to be described as " Alderman."

" Upon the day of St. Matthew the Apostle," a yearly court had to be held[1] for the election of the new Governors of the Hospital, and four days preceding this meeting these courteous communications passed :—

" 17° Septembris, 1649.

"The Gov'no[rs] present thought fit to direct and order that our Clarke, W[m] Cawthorne, shall attend upon M[r] Aldr'an Reynardson, who is chosen President of this Hospi[le] and know his pleasure and resolution, whether he will continue President and have his name certified as President the next Friday, being S[t] Mathewes Day, and alsoe when he will have a Co[rt] for the Hospi[le] wh : is desired to be a week or a fortnight after Michas. next; to this message our s[d] Clarke retorned this answere, That the s[d] late Alderman Reynardson retorned many thankes to the Gov'no[rs] for their love to him and desired to be excused that he had not bin with them before this tyme, fearcing that the business of the Hospi[le] had bin neglected by reason of his absence. But he desired to be excused to be President in respect he is often sick, and therefore could not doe that constant service that appteines to the place, but he would continue a Gov'nor of this House and doe what service he could for the poore."

During the Commonwealth there is no mention of Reynardson, save in the proceedings already given and on the MS. Records of the Merchant Taylors. New arms for the State were ordered at the Court of 28th August, 1650, to be set up for next Lord Mayor's Day, " according as the City and other Companies have done," but Reynardson was not present. On the 11th December Andrews (as Lord Mayor) ordered the removal of the " arms and pictures of the late King " from all churches and halls, and a certificate of such removal, so that on the 15th January the Master and Wardens of the Merchant Taylors' Company certified that they had caused to be

---

[1] Memoranda (1863), appendix, page 78.

taken down the arms and pictures[1] of the late King, which did remain standing in the Common Hall (*b*, page 580).

Although, as the outcome of the Rebellion, the Regal throne had been destroyed at Westminster, the Civic throne, resting on a popular basis, was upheld at Guildhall. The City continued to be governed by the Lord Mayor and Corporation, and the Guilds by the Masters and Wardens, for, by the Act of February, 1648,[2] every freeman was thereafter to be sworn to the Commonwealth of England,[3] and "to be obedient" to what the Act declared to be "the just and good government of the City of London," and "to maintain and preserve all the due franchises thereof."

These were thought by the Livery to be infringed on more than one occasion: the first being an attempt made to interfere with the rights of the Livery in the election of Lord Mayor and Sheriffs, when at the Court of October 20, 1650 (*b*) (Sir W. Acton and others being present), a petition was presented to the Court of Common Council, setting forth the rights of the Livery, in terms that are worth preserving:

" *The election* under the Act of the VII year of King Edward the III was by the Mayor and Aldermen, together with the most sufficient men of every ward. In the VIIIth year of the said King Edw[d] the III, as the King's Parliament then commanded, which was by the Aldermen and most discreet and ablest Citizens of the City. It in XX y[r] of the s[d] King by the Mayor and all the Aldermen and 12, 8, or 6 of every ward, according as the ward should be great or small, of the richest and wisest men of every ward. In the 50th y[r] of the s[d] King by a certain number of good men of the several mysteries, their names being certified by the several Companies.[4] In the 8th year of King Rich[d] the II by the Common Council and most sufficient men of the said City. In the 9th year of that King by those that shall be summoned of the most sufficient men of the City or of the Common Council. In the 7th year of King Edw[d] the IV, by the[5] C. C. M. and W. of every mystery of the City, coming in their Liveries, and by other good men specially summoned, so the said elections, continued in an unsettled manner until the 15th year of King Edward the IV, that the same election

---

[1] In 1672, Mr. John Short gave the Company a portrait of Charles I, which is in the Court Dining-room at the present day.

[2] Scobell, Part 2, page 4.

[3] *Ibid.*, c. 27, page 30.

[4] *Ibid.*, page 34.

[5] (*e*) "Common Council and Master and Wardens."

was settled by the authority of this Honble Court of C. C. by an Act then made that the M. & W. of the s^d Mysteries of this City, meeting in their Halls or other fit places, and associating with the good men of the Company, clothed in their best Liveries, should come together in the Guildhall of this City for the election of Mayor and Sheriffs, and that no other but the good men of the C. C. should be present at the s^d election," which the said Petitioners alleged "was the course and custom that had been ever since yearly used and continued for the honour, peace, and happiness of the s^d City of London, and the well-settled government of the same."

The appeal to the Common Council was for protection, and no Act, so far as I can trace (*a*), was made to their prejudice.

The other occasion was when an order was issued from the Lord Mayor, dated November 2, 1650, ordering the Master to summon each liveryman from his home, to appear before the Militia Committee at Guildhall on the 6th instant, by 8 A.M., to subscribe the engagement as directed by an order of Parliament, and the Masters and Wardens (*b*, page 364) were also to bring a roll of the names of the Clothing. It appears, on reference to the Corporation Records (*a*) of the 7th November, that this Order was met by a petition of remonstrance from all the Companies, and that no further action was taken against the Merchant Taylors.

So matters continued for some time, but at a subsequent period a "Committee of Corporations" sitting at the Queen's Court in Westminster, addressed a letter to the Merchant Taylors' Company, dated November 30, 1652, on the authority of a Parliamentary Order of the 14th September (*b*, page 409), requiring them to bring in their Charters on or before the 7th day of December, as the Committee judged it most agreeable with and suitable to the government of a commonwealth that they be held from and under the authority of the same.

Obedience was given to this Order so far as that the Wardens and Clerk were authorised to attend the Committee with the charters and true copies thereof, with an English translation, and to request permission to retain the charters to support their present Government, which, so far as I can trace, was granted, as the charters remain with the Company, and no surrender of them was ever made to the Commonwealth.

But, notwithstanding civil dissension was rampant outside, still inside the Hall the observance of old customs returned, furnishing an apt illustration how, as it has been well observed, the well-being of London has been "fostered by the kindly influence of civic hospitality." " Constantly in the habit of assembling at the festive board—as well in the greater Associations of the City as in the smaller bodies of the Guilds—our citizens, however much they might be at discord or variance, were always in the way of being brought together by good fellowship; and when," as Sir Francis Palgrave writes,[1] " rival parties abroad would have been employed in razing each other's property to the ground, our London factions united in demolishing the ramparts of a venison pasty." Thus on the 1st June, 1652, we have this entry :—

" After the business of the Court, then the Company resorted into the Hall, where, according to ancient custome the names of the Livery were called, and notice taken of such as were absent; then in a reverent manner praise[2] was made by one Mr. Abbott,[3] and afterwards the Ordinances of the house were openly read and also a great part of the booke of Benefactors; then preparation was made for dinner, whereunto were invited the Aldren of this Comp[le] and their wives, the whole Assistants and Livery, the old Masters' wives, the pres[t] Wardens' wives, the preacher Schoolm[r] and Warden Substitutes, and Almsmen of the Livery, as in ancient time hath been accustomed."[4]

Reynardson probably attended at this and other meetings until his death, for he was present in January, 1652, and on the 14th November, 1653, when the Lord Mayor's precept was received ' requiring the Company to line the streets on the occasion of His Highness the Protector and his Council dining at Grocers' Hall," and on the 20th of July, 1654, after which the Court Books are lost. As auditor he signed the cash books for the year 1655–56.

At the earliest stage of the Restoration he was not forgotten by his fellow citizens. Charles II, to gain the confidence of the City, had in April, 1660, addressed a letter to the Corporation,[5]

---

[1] The Merchant and the Friar, by Palgrave, London, 1844, page 70.

[2] All the Quarterly Courts were opened by prayer. The form of this in Henry VIIth's reign is printed at *j*, page 359, in Elizabeth's reign at *i*, page 128, and in James Ist's reign at page 130.

[3] This was probably Robert Abbott, a noted Puritan divine, then holding the rectory of St. Austin's, Watling Street, E.C. He was formerly curate of Worol Church, and though a Puritan was a thorough Churchman, against the Brownists, and a noble specimen of a clergyman.—Enc. Brit. (9th ed.), Vol. 1, page 25.

[4] *Ibid.*, pages 557–8.

[5] Clarendon, vol. 7, pages 462 —468.

enclosing " His Majesty's declaration as to the future measures for the pacification of existing troubles," but the Common Council appeared to think that, preliminary to all other matters, some " vindication of the conduct of the City " in the year of Reynardson's mayoralty was needed to restore the citizens to the respect and confidence of their fellow countrymen. Therefore on the 26th of April (a) a Committee of the Common Council was appointed to peruse the records and frame such; and on the 30th to a Court, fairly representative,[1] " a vindication "[2] was submitted and is thus recorded.

After setting out the endeavours of the City to bring about " a personal treaty with the King," and the entry of the soldiers into the House of Commons on the 7th [sic] of December, and the election of the Common Council, so " that nothing could rationally be expected to result from their debates but what was servile and horribly degenerative from the pristine honour of the City—*hinc illæ lacrymæ*—for on the 13th of January, being assembled in Common Council, they acted as follows." Then follows a verbatim account of those proceedings of the 13th and 15th which have been already given.

The vindication proceeds: " An act so abhorrent to all principles of Christianity and so nauxious to all men of sober principles that no comment can render it more odious, and, therefore, this Court cannot but declare their solemn protest on behalf of themselves and the generality of this City that they did then and still do abominate the same, and cannot omit to profess their thankful memory of the noble and gallant resolutions of the then Lord Mayor, *Alderman Reynardson*, and his brethren the Aldermen who so valiantly resisted the turbulent disorders of that mechanic juncto, during many hours' assault, and at last prudently retreated and washed their hands from the gilt of those bloody resolves; and as this Court doth hope that this preceeding narrative hath sufficiently vindicated it, and the generality of the City (with all

---

[1] Present:—

Thomas Aleyn, Lord Mayor, April 30, 1660.

Aldermen	Sir Thos. Atkin.	Wm. Bolton.	
	Sir Thos. Foote.	Wm. Wale.	
	Sir Thos. Viner.		
	Sir Christopher Pack.	Fras. Warner,	Aldermen and
	Anthony Bateman.	Wm. Love,	Sheriffs.

And more than 40 Councilmen.

[2] Printed by Jas. Flasher; presented to the Corporation, London, April 30, 1660.

F

impartial men) from the least suspicion of those rumours with which the world hath a long time been abused; so they doubt not but since the choice of the Common Council hath been put into any degree of freedom they have given sufficient testimony, that to their utmost of their capacity they have acted cordially and strenuously in order to the attainment of those blessed beginnings of re-establishment of these kingdoms, according to the motions of this present Parliament to whom they shall faithfully adhere and cheerfully submit, and as it hath been our prayer and endeavour for ourselves and the nation, so we trust we shall suddenly (by the good hand of God) and the wisdom of both Houses of Parliament be put under the protection of the just and fundamental government of hereditary and well-tempered monarchy, according to the ancient laws of the nation, and thereby reap a plentiful harvest of peace and joy for the long seed-time of tears that we have had."

The meetings of the Common Council from the 1st to the 8th of May were more or less continuous, and after communicating with the House of Commons, so as to act with their sanction, they appointed a Committee to frame instructions for a deputation and to name the members who should as such attend the King. An addition to both was made on the 4th by adding Mr. Alderman Reynardson thereto; but, though aged and infirm in health, he sought not as another did[1] an exemption from this duty, which was to be discharged at the individual cost and charge of the deputation, as ordered by the Common Council.

We are indebted to Clarendon[2] for an account of this meeting. "The King" (so he writes) "was waited upon by 14 of the most substantial citizens, who assured His Majesty of their fidelity and most cheerful submission, and that they placed all their felicity and hope of future prosperity in the assurance of his grace and favour." The Corporation books only mention the return of the deputation, and that the Recorder made a verbal report to the Common Council on the 28th of May, (a) who by resolution gave the deputation, whose names are not given, "hearty thanks for their great pains and charges therein." Whitelock states that the King knighted the deputation. (h)

The King entered the City on the 29th of May (his birthday),

---

[1] I presume he went, because he sought no exemption, but it is doubtful.

[2] Vol. 7, page 500.

and was received by the Lord Mayor and principal citizens, led on by Major-General Browne to a tent pitched with sumptuous magnificence in St. George's Place, Southwark.[1] The old-fashioned civic hospitality soon found an occasion for its display, as, on the 5th of July, the King and his Court were entertained at the Guildhall, where, in the withdrawing-room, Reynardson was knighted.[2]

As we have already seen, he was not forgotten by his fellow citizens, and on the 4th of September, was restored to office as Alderman by the Common Council. At the coming election of Lord Mayor what more fitting than that they should testify their supreme respect for him by electing him as the first Lord Mayor of the Restoration? This they did, but, as in the case of his former election, no entry whatever is to be found of it in the Corporation Records.

I have not searched to ascertain whether similar omissions are frequent, but the Lord Mayor's procession on St. Simon's and St. Jude's Day was and is a " proclamation " of the elected civic ruler for the year, both necessary in itself and far more effective than if made by the " heralds ": his person and, as bearing with him the mace and sword, his authority thus became known to those over whom he was about to exercise supreme civic sovereignty.

Of the fact of his election the Common Council Records furnish this proof: " At a meeting of the Common Council of the 1st of October, 1660—Read a letter from Sir Abraham Reynardson, Knight, Lord Mayor Elect for this City, for the year ensuing, thereby declaring his sickly condition and inability by reason thereof for the execution of so weighty a place. Withal returning his thanks to this City for their love showed to him therein, and desiring that they would be pleased to bestow the same favour upon a fitter person for that service. This Court, taking the same into consideration and likewise that the said Sir A. Reynardson had formerly undergone the execution of the s^d place of Lord Mayor for the space of half a year, did think fit to grant his request, and do order that the same Sir A. Reynardson be discharged from the s^d place of Lord Mayor of this City for the year ensuing." (a)

We may now revert to one of the subsequent incidents of

---

[1] Echard (1717), vol. 2, page 409.
[2] Herbert in his Book of Knights has no entry of Reynardson, but see London Pageants, by Nichol (1831), page 73.

Browne's life, viz., his connection with the Merchant Taylors' Company, and his succession to the Mayoralty in 1660. During the Commonwealth no favour was shown to him, and he was released from prison only after a long imprisonment. After his release he was active in forwarding the Restoration, being anxious that it should be brought about rather through the agency of Fleetwood than of Monk; but when the King came he was, as we shall see, one of the foremost among the citizens to welcome him.

The successor to Reynardson as Lord Mayor was Sir Thomas Browne, who before his election must have been admitted to the Merchant Taylors' Company by redemption. However, the facts are certain (though our records at least cannot be cited), for "the Pageant of the Royal Oak,"[1] by John Tatham, as performed at the cost and charge of the Company, is extant. Pepys went to see his house near Goldsmiths' Hall, and to the "Key" at Cheapside to see this show. He is entered as attending the Court of Assistants on the 14th July, 1664, but he never served any office in the Company other than that of Assistant.[2]

The recorded incidents of Reynardson's life cease from this period. Notwithstanding his losses as a Royalist, his life was a prosperous one, for, besides an accumulation of personal property, he had acquired lands in Essex and Sussex, in addition to his manor house at Tottenham.

His will is dated on the 10th of May, 1661,[3] and witnessed by his friend George Smallwood. "Wherever he dwelt at the time of his death he desired to be buried at St. Martin's Outwich, under the pew or seat where he was last seated." "His funeral," which, as that of an Alderman who had passed the Chair, might otherwise have been held at midnight, "was to be at about three o'clock in the afternoon, with the children of Christ's Hospital as choristers,[4] and

---

[1] Fairholt's Pageants, part 2, page 89.

[2] See his life, vol. 4, pages 54 and 192, D. of N. B. His portrait in Ricraft, page 1070, and Grainger, vol. 3, page 77, 1 ed., 1824.

[3] Proved in London, October 22, 1661.

[4] The terms of this bequest were: "50*l.* to Christ's Hospital for their relief and their boys going to church with my corps."

For some years after the establishment of Christ's Hospital the boys attended the burials of distinguished citizens or benefactors (Machyn's Diary, page 32), and the fees paid were a source of income (see Burials, in the early accounts of the hospital). To improve their singing, Robert Dowe (*j*, page 107) established a school for singing, which is still in existence. The hospital received in 1662–63 —exclusive of Reynardson's gift of 50*l.*—41*l.* in fees of 5*l.* to 10*l.*, and in 1663–64 21*l.* in fees of 4*l.* to 8*l.*

to be attended by the Livery of his Company and such of his parishioners and friends as might be minded thereto." To the same Company he gave 300*l.* as a pension fund for six poor women of the Company,[1] and "as a further token of his love to the Company bequeathed to them 140 ounces of silver made into a basin and ewer, to be used at their usual feasts, whereon should be set his name and arms or some inscription in remembrance of him as donor."

Unfortunately the Merchant Taylors' records for this period are lost, and we have to look to other sources[2] for the date of his death and funeral. He died at Tottenham on the 4th of October, and his corpse was carried to the Merchant Taylors' Hall, where it lay in state until the 17th, covered with one or other of those beautiful hearse cloths still to be seen there, and which are elsewhere described by Mr. A. W. Franks, C.B., F.S.A.[3] The funeral was under the direction of the Heralds, three of whom, Lancaster, Chater, and Somerset, attended, and all the Civic Authorities were present.[3] Thus, with

"that which should accompany old age,
As honour, love, obedience, troops of friends,"

this worthy citizen was laid to his rest. His widow, who survived him, having made her will on the 17th of June, 1673,[4] died, and was buried on the 14th July, 1674, in the chancel under the pews numbered 4 and 3,[5] but no monument was erected to either of them.

Their remains were undisturbed until the church was pulled down in 1874,[6] prior to which the floor was dug out to a depth of 14 feet to insure that no human remains were left therein,[7] and these were removed to the City of London Cemetery at Ilford, where a monument was erected over them with this inscription :—

---

[1] *i*, page 329. The plate was probably lost in the fire of 1666, as it is not now owned by the Company.

[2] Robinson, page 103.

[3] Appendix III.

[4] Proved February 15, 1675.

[5] Parish Register. There is a print of the interior of the old church in Wilkinson (London, 1797).

[6] The last service was held June 22, 1873. The Capital and Counties Bank now occupies the site.

[7] To give some idea of the extent to which burials were made within church walls, it may be mentioned that "115 coffins and 112 large cases of bones" were exhumed and removed to Ilford, the work occupying the whole of January and February, 1874."—MS. of Mr. Nathaniel Stephens (parish clerk) of the M. T. C.

Sacred
to
The memory of
Eighteen Generations
of the Parishioners of
St. Martin Outwich
in the City of London
who died in the Lord and were
buried within the walls of
their Parish Church
and whose remains were on the
union of their Parish Church with that of
St. Helen's Bishopsgate
removed to this Cemetery
by order of the Queen in Council.
A.D. 1874.
JOHN BATHURST DEANE, M.A., Rector.[1]

JOHN CHASE CRADDOCK,   } Churchwardens.
WILLIAM HENRY JANSON,   }
A.D. 1876.
" These are the dead which die in the Lord."

There are two portraits extant of Reynardson as Lord Mayor:
one at Merchant Taylors' Hall and another at Holywell Hall.
Both portraits are the same in style and treatment.   He is represented in the gown and chain of office with the mace and sword
lying beside him.   His hair is brown, tinged with grey, and a
picked grey beard, his right hand hanging down, the forefinger of
his left supporting a pearl drop pendant from his chain, and on the
little finger is a ring with a red stone.   His short coat is red, laced
with gold, and the sleeves are turned up with laced ruffles.[2]   His
wife Eleanor's portrait is by Cornelius Jansen, 1648.

Looking at the scant record of his life here presented, and to
the memoir of him given by his friend George Smallwood, it is
surely certain that Reynardson was a man of such characteristics
that the Company may well be proud of him.   He was a stanch
Churchman and a loyal citizen when many around him dared

---

[1] Mr. Deane, F.S.A., was well known to many of us as the author of "The
Worship of the Serpent" (2nd ed.), London, 1833, and "The Life of Richard
Deane," both of which works he very kindly presented to me.

[2] Robinson, vol. 1, page 105.

not to be either. His attachment to the Church is shown by his gift of Communion plate and his testamentary direction as to the place of his burial. His loyalty to the Crown is evidenced by his suffering degradation, fine, and imprisonment, rather than abandon his allegiance, and when this tyranny had been overcome he was held in "thankful memory" by his fellow-citizens "for his noble and gallant resolution" in withstanding the Rump.

Nor was he less attached to his Guild, although in its membership some were to be found foremost in the ranks of the Rebellion, and one placed his seal to the warrant for the King's execution. He made the Guild the almoners of his charity, and remembering the social amenities which, despite political differences, he had enjoyed in the Common Hall with his brother guildsmen, he bequeathed, " as a token of his love to them," "a bason and ewer to be used by them at their usual feasts."

If therefore it be incumbent upon us "to praise famous men," this guildsman deserves some memorial, "for he was a merciful man and one whose righteousness ought not to be forgotten."

As to the family of Reynardson, some of them lingered in the parish for many years, Francis and Sarah Reynardson being buried in the chancel of the church on the 29th of January, 1739; but, strange as it may seem, we do not trace that any of his family were ever admitted to the membership of the Merchant Taylors' Company, although his will directed that "his sons should be brought up in the art or course of merchandize."[1] His brother's widow fell into poor circumstances, and was a pensioner in 1681.[2]

The family is at present represented by the "Birch-Reynardsons" of Holywell Hall, Stamford, who stand in Bateman's "Great Landowners"[3] as owning 6,004 acres in Lincolnshire and 40 acres in Rutland. One of his descendants commanded the Grenadier Guards at the battle of Inkerman in 1854.

---

[1] His son Nicholas, in his will, April 2, 1685 (proved March 2, 1689), styles himself "Citizen and M. T.," as he was by birth.

[2] 1681, March 24, Vol. 12, fol. 187.—"It is thought fit and so ordered that Mary Vaux, one of Sir Abraham Reynardson's pensioners, whose last husband was not free of this Company and thereby not capable of the said pension, be discharged of her said pension, but in consideration of her poverty and her last husband being brother to the s⁴ Sir Abraham Reynardson, doth think fit and so order that the Master of this Compy for the time being do pay unto her quarterly 6s. 8d. out of the Poor Box during her natural life, the first payment to be made for Lady Day last, and for the Master's so doing this order to be his discharge."

[3] Page 379.

APPENDIX I.

ON THE ELECTION OF LORD MAYOR AND SHERIFFS.

Any of the offices in the Corporation to which a citizen is eligible, and to which he is duly elected, he must accept, and discharge its duties at his own cost (which at times has been ruinous to the officers) or suffer the penalty of his disobedience (*j*, page 25).[1] Thus Fitz William, elected Sheriff in 1520, but not serving, was disfranchised;[2] and Sir Thomas White, elected Alderman in 1533–34, but refusing to serve, was committed to Newgate.[3]

An early instance of election of a Mayor by choice is given in 1441–42, when Clapton (the Draper) was preferred to Ralph Holland (the Merchant Taylor).[4]

And no doubt the citizens have the right of choosing their Mayors and Sheriffs, and, in times of political crises, have freely exercised it. Before the adoption of Parliamentary government in 1689, contests, as in 1682–83, between the Crown and the citizens not unfrequently arose as to the election of the Sheriffs and Lord Mayor.

The history of these in 1682–83 is set out in the pages of Echard:[5] here it is sufficient to give only a sketch.

At the election of Sheriffs in 1681–82 the King, acting through the then Lord Mayor (Sir John Moore), insisted on the return of North and Rich, the Court candidates, against Papillion and Dubois, chosen by the Livery. The returning officers, the Sheriffs Pilkington and Shute were charged with riot,[6] and tried at the Old Bailey. Pilkington[7] was then sued by the Duke of York for slander, and 100,000*l*. recovered against him for damages. At the trial of this action, Sir Patience Ward,[8] of the Merchant Taylors'

---

[1] *j*, vol. 2, p. 135, note 2.

[2] *Ibid.*, page 45.

[3] *Ibid.*, page 102.

[4] *Ibid.*, vol. 1, page 135.

[5] Vol. 3, book 4, page 363.

[6] *k*, vol. 9, page 187. Ward's trial is at page 298.

[7] Pilkington was elected Lord Mayor on Chapman's death in March, 1688, and was re-elected for 1689 and for 1690, being two and a half years in office.

[8] Sir Patience Ward was the son of Thomas Ward, of Tonshelfe, in the county of York, Gentleman, and apprenticed to Lancelot Tolson, Merchant, of St. Helen's, June 10, 1646, and made free by his master, September 24, 1655. On November 10, 1670, as Sheriff and Alderman, he was sworn an Assistant; June 30, 1671, elected

Company, gave evidence for the defendant; and was afterwards indicted for perjury, but never sentenced.

At the election of Lord Mayor for 1682–83, Sir William Pritchard,[1] of the Merchant Taylors' Company, was the senior Alderman, and opposed by the anti-Court party, who put forward against him Alderman Goold. The contest was so severe that his election was gained by 14 votes only (2138—2124).

These contests provoked Charles II to take that ill-advised measure of filing an information against the Corporation to invalidate their charters, which were ultimately restored to them by

---

Master; 1681, Lord Mayor. He owned part of the original mansion in Suffolk Lane, which Richard Hilles did not purchase in 1561, but which part the M. T. C. in recent years have acquired. There was some hesitation on his part in taking up his livery, and he was summoned before the Court of Assistants, and this decision was recorded on June 10, 1663 :—

"Whereas Patience Ward, a Merchant Taylor, in Laurence Pountney Lane, hath oftentimes been summoned to this Court to be admitted into the Livery and Clothing of this Society, and hath sometimes appeared accordingly and desired time to consider thereof, but on his last appearance refused either to accept of the Livery or fine for the same. Whereupon it was ordered that the said Patience Ward should be summoned to appear before the next Court of Aldermen or to sue him upon the Ordinance of this house to compel him thereunto at such time as our Master think fit. But our Master, out of his especial favour unto him, and upon information that he had considered thereof, did cause him to be summoned to this Court, who appeared accordingly and humbly desired that this Court would be pleased to spare him until the next call, and then he would serve them either in purse or person, or both. Whereupon and after serious debate thereof, and because he should see that the Company desired as well his company as his money, it is ordered that he should presently pay 50*l.* to the use of this Society, and if he shall please to accept of the Livery at any time within a year now next ensuing, then he shall have what shall be over and above of the usual fine now paid by every member admitted the Livery repaid him and be ranked in the Livery as if he now accepted of the same, or else he shall be for the said 50*l.* discharged from being admitted into the Clothing and Livery of this Society."

However, he was not in circumstances to pay 50*l.* to the Company, and upon the motion of Sir William Bolton, in November, "It was ordered that our Master do accept of 40*l.* in money in part of the 50*l.* which Mr. Patience Ward oweth this Company for his fine to be excused from all offices of this Company (except Master), and the other 10*l.*, being the remainder of the said 50*l.*, to be laid out and bestowed in buying such books towards furnishing the Library belonging to the Company's grammar school at Laurance Pountney, London, as Mr. John Goad, chief school-master there, shall direct and appoint."

[1] On October 6, 1647, William Pritchard, son of Francis Pritchard, of the borough of Southwark, Ropemaker, was apprenticed to Abraham Manco, of Southwark, and on August 22, 1655, was made free by his master. He was admitted to Livery between 1659 and 1663, but the records and account books during these years are lost. On August 16, 1672, as lately elected Sheriff and Alderman of London, he was admitted an Assistant; and July 10, 1673, as Sheriff and Alderman, elected Master of the Company. He was Lord Mayor, 1682; will dated December 29, 1702; will proved, April 17, 1705.

William III. Since the year 1689, these contests with the Crown, save for a few years in George III's reign, have ceased; and the rule of seniority, with few exceptions, has prevailed.

In the year 1738–39 political feeling was greatly excited against Sir Robert Walpole for his policy with Spain, and the Livery were invited " to assert[1] their ancient right of free choice, and drop the absurd modern practice of rotation," and they did so. The senior Alderman set aside was Sir George Champion, the M.P. for Aylesbury, who supported[2] Walpole. Against what he deemed to be a great personal injustice, he protested in a letter on 22nd September, addressed to the Livery, setting forth that by their reversing the established order of election all the expensive preparations which he had already made for the dignity and grandeur of the station would be rendered useless (*f*, page 1243). However, public feeling[3] was too strong for him, and Sir John Salter,[4] of the Merchant Taylors' Company, was chosen for the mayoralty. In later years Sir George Champion was again passed over, and in 1740 the rule of seniority was infringed, for the Livery returned Sir Robert Godshall to the Court of Aldermen as the senior Alderman ; but they, contrary to custom, nominated George Heathcote, the second candidate, who excused himself from service, and received the thanks of the Common Hall for declining in support of the liberties of the city.[5] The Livery then returned Godshall, with Humphrey Parsons, the senior Alderman above the chair, and after three hours' debate, Parsons was chosen by 12 to 11 votes, and served the office.

From 1754 to 1765 the rule of seniority prevailed ; but in each year from 1766 to 1775 there was a contest, and a departure from the order of seniority. In 1776, and later years, seniority has been observed, and when the Lord Mayor was presented for the King's approval in 1777, the Lord Chancellor " congratulated the City on a return of that dignity, peace, and tranquility which had

---

[1] Gent's Mag., vol. 9, page 495.
[2] Mahon's Eng., vol. 3, page 17.
[3] See reasons for and against his election, London, 1739, Guild. Cat., page 166.
[4] On March 2, 1710, John Salter, son of Thomas Salter, made free by patrimony on report of Samuel Cugley, Esq., and Mr. John Cooper of the Court, and admitted on the Livery, pursuant to an order of the last Court, and excused all offices except Master for the fine of 20*l.*, and took the usual oath of a liveryman. On October 15, 1730, he was sworn an Assistant on his election as Alderman, and July 8, 1731, was elected Master. He was Sheriff in 1735, and Lord Mayor in 1739. His will is dated April 23, 1736, and proved August 1, 1744.
[5] Gent's Mag., vol. 10, page 468.

been lost and disturbed for many years, and expressed a hope that matters would return to the old channel."[1]

I may mention that the Company possess portraits of the three Merchant Taylor Aldermen referred to in this note.

APPENDIX II.

FUNERAL CERTIFICATE.[2]

The Right Worshipfull Sr Abraham Reynardson, Knight, Alderman of London, departed this life at his house at Tottenham, in Middx: on Friday the 4th of October, 1661, from whence his corps was removed to Merchantaylors Hall in London, and there (sett out with all ceremonies belonging to his degree) remained till Thursday 17th of the same October, and then was carryed thence to the Parish Church of St Martin Outwich in Bishopgate Streete, London, and there interred. The Lord Mayor and Aldermen, the Governours, Deputies, and Assistants of the Turky and East India Companies, the Livery of the Company of Merchantaylors, and the Governors of St Bartholomews Hospitall, with a very great number of his relations and acquaintance attending thither. The said defunct was Lord Mayor of London in the yeare 1649, but was by the then pretended Parliament discharged from his mayoralty and disabled to beare the office of Mayor and Alderman of London, fined 2,000*l.*, and committed to prison for refuseing to proclaim their trayterous act for abollishing the kingly office in England, the said fine was levyed by the sale of his goods by the candle. The said defunct had two wives. The first, Abigall, one of the daughters and coheires of Nicholas Crispe, of London, Esqr, by whome he had issue, Nicholas, their only child now living. The second wife was Elianor, daughter of Richard Wynne, of Shrewsbury, in the county of Salop, Esqr, by whome he had issue three sonnes and three daughters, living at the time of his decease, Samuell eldest, Isaac second, and Jacob third, sonnes, Mary, eldest daughter, the wife of Samuell Bernardiston, Merchant, Priscilla the second, and Abigal the third daughters, both unmarried at the time of his decease. The Officers of Arms that directed and attended the

---

[1] Ann. Regis., vol. 20, page 208.
[2] I am indebted to Colonel Birch-Reynardson for this certificate.

solemnity were William Ryley Lancaster, Thomas Lee Chester, and Thomas St. George, Somersett Heralds of Armes. This certificate was taken by the said Thomas Lee the twelveth day of January, 1661.

THOMAS LEE, CHESTER.

APPENDIX III.

MEMOIR BY GEORGE SMALLWOOD, M.A.

And now let me crave your patience a little longer, to speak a few words of the occasion of our present meeting; though it is not my custome to make large Panegyricks, or commendatory Orations at the Funerals of the dead, because I know the comfort of a sincere Christian is, *That his praise is not of men, but of God.*

Yet for example and encouragement to others, I cannot but speak something of this worthy and Heroick Citizen, Sir *Abraham Raynardson*, Knight, late Alderman, and sometime Lord Mayor of this honorable City of *London*, upon whom my Text is a fit Commentary, and I am perswaded may be truly applied to his practice: For as far as I was able to judge by the course of his conversation, for those many years acquaintance which I had with him, and the experience I had of him, I think I may truly say of him, he was one that sowed righteousness.

For as to his life and conversation, he always appeared to me, and I think to all others that knew him, to be very innocent and inoffensive; a man of a very strict life, walking as it was said of *Zachary* and *Elizabeth*, in all the Ordinances and Commandments of God, though not ἀναμάρτητος, without sin, for who walk so; yet ἄμεμπτος, without blame: No man, as I ever heard, could justly charge anything upon him.

1. As for his piety to God, he was a man Orthodox and sound in the Faith, not tainted with any Heretical opinion, or drawn away from the truth established amongst us, as too many have been in this time of Apostacy: He was a diligent and constant attender upon the publick Ordinances upon the Lords dayes, a carefull observer of holy Duties in his Family, and as I have been informed, his closet was conscious to his secret devotions: He was a man of few words, and affected not, as many do, εὐ

προσωπῆσαι ἐν σαρκὶ, to make a fair shew in the flesh, and to say with *Jehu*, come see my zeal for the Lord of hosts : but I am perswaded by all probabilities, he was constant in putting up his suits and supplications at the Throne of grace in secret, remembring our Saviours counsel, Matth. 6. 6. " Thou, when thou prayest, enter into thy Closet, and when thou hast shut thy door, pray to thy Father which is in secret, and thy Father which seeth in secret shall reward thee openly :" this I have reason to think was his practice.

2. For his relations ; he was a loving Husband, and a careful Father, one that not onely made good provision for their outward estate by his industry in his Calling, and Gods blessing upon it, but was also carefull of the welfare of their souls ; witness the good admonitions and counsels to his Children upon his Death-bed, which I hope will make such an impression upon their Spirits, as shall not easily be forgotten, *viz.* to be constant in calling upon the Name of God, and to serve him faithfully ; to be dutifull and obedient to their Mother, and to live in love and unity one with another. The Lord grant them grace to remember and practice these things, and follow their deceased Fathers advice, as the *Rechabites* did the counsel of their father *Jonadab*, that the blessing of God may rest upon them.

3. For his dealing with men, he was very carefull to sowe this seed of righteousness, he was very exact and just in all his dealings, oppressing no man, defrauding no man, as I hope all that he dealt with can bear witness. I never heard the least blemish cast upon him in this respect: and this is no mean commendation. We finde nothing more pressed in Scripture than righteous dealing with men, and nothing more condemned then the contrary. God saith, " He hath shewed thee, O man, what is good, and what doth the Lord require of thee, but to do justly, and to love mercy, and to walk humbly with thy God," Mich. 6. 8. The wise man telleth us, " That a false ballance is abomination to the Lord : but a just weight is his delight," Prov. 11. 1. This is the voice of God throughout the Scriptures, he had rather no sacrifices should be offered upon his altar, than that they should be the fruits of wrong and violence : he professeth plainly, " I the Lord love judgement, I hate robbery for burnt-offering," Isa. 61. 8.

Indeed it is no true piety that is separated from justice and honesty, nor real honesty if it be divided from true piety : he that seemeth to be zealous in the duties of Religion, and yet makes no conscience of his dealings with men, is but a glorious hypocrite :

and he that dealeth justly with men, and hath no due care of the duties of piety to God, is but au honest Infidel; both joyned together make a sincere Christian; and such a one I am perswaded was this worthy Knight.

4. For his mercy and liberality to the poor, he did not blow a Trumpet before his alms-deeds, neither shall I; onely thus much I can say, his hands were opened to the necessities of the poor, and those of the place where he lived are sensible that they have lost a good Benefactor. The stream of his bounty did run chiefly in one Channel, *viz.* in taking poor children, and placing them in such Callings, wherein they might get their own bread, and provide things honest in the sight of men. This was a very good work, au odour of a sweet smell, yet this was not all, the beams of his charity did shine upon other objects while he lived, and as the Sun after his setting casts some light above the Horizon; so now his Sun is set, some beames of his charity will appear to the comfort of the poor in the several Hospitals of this City, and some other places.

5. But then the greatest and most eminent Tryall and Testimony of his Righteousness and Integrity was in that fatal year 1648, when the Blood of His Sacred Majesty was shed by cruel and wicked hands, then it pleased God to call him to be Lord Mayor of *London ;* in which office coming to him in such a stormy time, he was stedfast and unmoveable from his Integrity, he shewed himself a good Christian, a wise Magistrate, a loyal Subject, and a loving Citizen.

Indeed *Magistratus indicat virum,* Magistracy is a touchstone which will discover a man whether he be gold or dross: he that carrieth himself as he ought in Offices of eminency, giveth a great testimony of his wisdom and virtue: There are two things that commend a Magistrate, Honesty and Courage, both these were eminent in him. There were three very memoriable passages to be observed in this worthy Knight, in managing his publick affairs.

1. In reference to the good of the City, whereof he was chief Magistrate when a Treaty was concluded upon, between His late Majesty of Blessed Memory, and the Parliament then sitting, and in order thereunto, an ingagement was subscribed by most of the Common Council, and principal Members of the City, for the carrying on of that Treaty. Afterwards the Treaty proving ineffectual, and the Parliament being dissolved by the unjust violence of the Army and their Abetters, a strict inquiry was made after the names of those that subscribed the personal Treaty: But the

Book wherein the names of the Subscribers on both parts, for and against the Treaty were written, containing about two Reams of Paper, being privately brought to this worthy Knight then Lord Mayor, he tendering the good and welfare of all his Brethren and fellow citizens, not knowing what might be the evil consequence of it, if such a Record should be found extant, took it and burnt it to ashes privately in his Chamber, that nothing might remain to the prejudice of any ; how many perhaps here present were deeply ingaged to him for the safety of their estates, if not of their lives, by that one action ? certainly it was a work full of wisdom, charity, and brotherly kindness : a most excellent concatenation of Christian Graces.

2. When some tumultuous and busie Commoners had contrived a traiterous and wicked Petition to bring His Sacred Majesty and others to a Tryal, and were vehemently urgent to have it read and voted in the Common-council, that so it might be presented to the then new moulded Parliament, as the desire of the whole City : This Heroick and Noble Knight stoutly opposed the promoting thereof, and would suffer it neither to be read nor voted, notwithstanding the rage and violence of the adverse party, who neither reverencing the Authority of his venerable office, nor regarding the gravity of his person, loaded him with reproach and contempt within, telling him they would have it voted whether he would or no before their rising ; and some of them stirred up a tumultous Rabble against him without : Notwithstanding all this unworthy dealing with him, he continued like an unmoveable Rock, persisting in his resolution, and endured those insolencies from eight of the clock in the morning until after eight at night, accompanied only with two of his brethren, and would not yield a jot to their unreasonable desires, notwithstanding all their clamorous importunities. And at last when no reason would prevaile with them, not able longer to endure their uncivil behaviour towards him, and chiefly that he might to the utmost of his power keep the City and Citizens from being stained with the guilt of that Sacred Innocent Blood, he resolutely took up the Sword, and departed the Court to his great hazzard. All these proceedings he caused to be registred in the book of Records belonging to the City for an evident testimony to after times, of his own and the Cities Integrity and Innocency as to that ungodly and execrable Fact of taking away the Kings Life, which he heartily abhorred : for all which noble and gallant resolutions and performances, he had since publick thanks given him by a declaration from the City.

Thus this worthy Knight might well be called the Sword and Buckler of *London*, as *Camillus* and *Fabius* were among the *Romans*, for he defended them from that which is worse than any outward evil, *viz.* from blood guiltiness, and that in the highest degree, even from the guilt of parracide, and shedding the blood of him that was *Pater Patriæ*, the Father of their Country. This was a great mercy to the City on Gods part, and an eminent favour on his part that did it, and the whole City have cause to be thankfull to God and him for it. When the rest of the children of *Israel* understood that their brethren the children of *Reuben*, the children of *Gad*, and the Children of *Manasseh* had not turned from following the Lord, by building an Altar for Burnt-Offerings besides the Altar of the Lord their God, which was before his Tabernacle, but only had built a pattern of the Lords Altar, to be a witness between them and their brethren, that they and their posterity belonged to the Congregation of Israel, and had a part in the Lord and his Service, as well as the other Tribes ; when they understood the Truth of this, it is said, the thing pleased them, and they blessed God, and said, "This day we perceive that the Lord is among us, because ye have not committed this trespass against the Lord : now ye have delivered the children of Israel out of the hand of the Lord," Joshua 22. 31. They rejoyced that God had kept their brethren from polluting themselves with that crying sin of Idolatry, and turning from the Lord and his Altar, and took it as a token of Gods presence among them, and as a merciful deliverance of the whole Nation, from the avenging hand of God and his fierce wrath, which the guilt of that sin would have brought upon them : Truly we in this City have great cause to be well pleased, and to bless God as well as they, for keeping us from being guilty of His Majesties Blood ; we have reason to interpret this happy providence as they did, to be a pledge and token that God would not forsake us, but continue his gracious presence among us, as blessed be his name he is pleased to do, as we see at this day, and I hope through mercy shall still see, as also to be a merciful deliverance of this City from the fearful wrath and severe vengeance of the most righteous God, which the guilt of that Sacred Blood, besides its other crying abominations would have brought upon it; we have reason to magnifie God for that gracious deliverance, and for raising up this worthy Knight to be so happily instrumental therein : had it been some faint hearted *Ephraimite*, or covetous *Demas*, he would have turned back in the day of battail, and for want of Christian courage, would have betraied this City into the hands of her enemies, and consequently have exposed her to the wrath of God; but this noble *Heroe* stood stoutly in defiance of all opposition, was couragious and faithful to his trust, and would not betray it for fear of men, or love of this present world.

3. When the then usurping Parliament had made an Act to abolish the Kingly Office and House of Lords, and sent it to this worthy Person then Lord Mayor to be proclaimed at the usual places of the City, he judging it altogether inconsistent with nay, positively, contrary to, the several oaths which he had taken, and considering of what dangerous consequence it might be to the City and Citizens, he delayed to do it for eight days, and afterward being summoned to come in person before the Parliament, to give a reason of his refusal, he appearing, told them plainly, that his conscience being forecharged with divers oaths, would not permit him to do what they required. Though he was before so great an Assembly, surrounded with his enemies, and his person, estate, liberty, and life were all in their power, and lay at their mercy, which was no better than cruelty, yet he did not shrink back for fear, but gave them a flat denial to their very faces; whereupon he was voted out of his Office, fined Two thousand pound, and committed Prisoner to the Tower of *London*, where he remained for a time, and was afterwards released: but not paying his fine, the Committee for advance of monies, ordered his goods, housholds stuff, and wearing apparel to be sequestred and sold by a candle, which was done accordingly, and so his whole fine was extorted from him in Money, Bonds, and Goods, by the power of that Committee.

Thus the unspotted Integrity and Christian fortitude of this then Honourable Lord Mayor did shine forth most gloriously in the midst of his persecutions and afflictions, like the Stars in a clear cold frosty night, to the honour of God and the Example of others; he suffered for His Majesty, he suffered for the Nobility, he suffered for the City and his fellow Citizens, and in all these, which is his greatest happiness, and the greatest shame to his enemies, he suffered persecution for Righteousness, and to keep a good conscience, and such our Saviour pronounceth blessed, and saith, " That great is their Reward in Heaven," Mat. 5. 12. In expectation of this reward he would rather hazzard his Estate, Liberty, Life, and all that was dear and precious to him, than defile his conscience and break his Oath, which was lawfull for the matter, and lawfully imposed for the Authority.

O if men had been so conscionable in those days in keeping

the lawful Oathes which they had taken, our land had not been so stained with the blood of her own children, neither had we seen and felt those Miseries and Calamities under which this City and Nation groaned for so many years together. The Lord of his infinite mercy give repentance and pardon for all the perjury of these perillous times.

Our Christian Worthy would have no share in it, nothing to burthen his conscience nor disturb his peace; he was firm and inflexible in his Resolution, and as *St. Jerome* saith of *Joseph*, he was not changed from his Uprightness and Integrity, *nec squalore carceris, nec tumore Ægyptiæ potestatis*, neither by the unsavouriness of a Prison, nor by the Pride and Swelling of that Egyptian power then in being : he was a man so carefull to sow Righteousness, that he was well content with the fruits of Gods Blessing upon his endeavors in his lawful calling, and never sought to add one penny to his estate, or inrich himself by the spoils and ruines of others, like Harpies and Crows that love to feed upon dead carkeises, and to eat the fruits of other mens labours. And which was none of the meanest of Gods mercies to him, the Lord was pleased to keep him from having any hand in beginning or promoting our late unnatural troubles and commotions : he was a man of very peaceable and quiet Spirit, which in the sight of God is of great price, he was none of the Sons of *Mars*, none of those people that delight in War, but he heartily wished and prayed for the welfare of our *Sion*, and the peace of our *Jerusalem :* this was one special favour of God to him, to keep him from having fellowship with the unfruitful works of darkness, according to that Song of *Hannah*, "He will keep the feet of his Saints, and the wicked shall be silent in darkness, for by strength shall no man prevaile," 1 Sam. 2. 9. But his fidelity and love of peace, were very costly to him (though indeed such a purchase as the reward of Righteousness, cannot be bought at too dear a rate) for his being Lord Mayor that year, was prejudicious to his Estate at least to the value of Twenty thousand pound, besides his Fine, as he hath affirmed under his own hand, and I dare believe it, coming from the mouth or pen of a person of such Worth and Integrity as he was.

And for all these sufferings he hath no recompence upon earth, but we may very fitly apply that of the Preacher to his condition, Eccles. 9. 14, 15, "There was a little City, and few men within it ; and there came a great King against it, and besieged it, and built great bulwarks against it : now there was found in it a poor wise man, and he by his wisdom delivered the City, yet no man remembred that same poor man." This is very suitable to our present purpose, except in some circumstances : I confess there is some difference in this place from that, and in this person from that, for this City is great, and there are many men in it, and this person was rich and not poor, but the work and recompence of both, run Parrallel, for this wise and righteous man delivered the City by his wisdom and righteousness, yet no man remembred this same wise and righteous man. It is pity such honorable worthy Christian actions as these should not be proportionably regarded and rewarded upon earth. But this is the comfort of the righteous man, and it is unspeakable, that his reward is with God in Heaven, yea God himself is his exceeding great reward.

This worthy Knight sowed Righteousness, and I hope that through the infinite mercies of God, and invaluable merits of the Lord Jesus Christ, upon whom alone he relied for Justification and Salvation, that he hath received this sure reward, which shall never be taken from him : the Lord give us grace so to follow the steps of his Integrity and Stedfastness in believing and well doing, that we may have a sure reward with the Generation of the Righteous in Gods Heavenly Kingdom, *Amen.*

HARRISON AND SONS, PRINTERS IN ORDINARY TO HER MAJESTY, ST. MARTIN'S LANE.

www.ingramcontent.com/pod-product-compliance
Lightning Source LLC
Chambersburg PA
CBHW020032030726
47499CB00007B/2393